INSOMNIA

INSOMNIA

TEE SEABRONE

DEDICATION

To everyone who has ever dreamed of a world where poetic justice could be served piping hot, but the law said, "Not so fast!"—this book is for you. May your creative solutions to life's injustices always stay just within the bounds of legality.

CHAPTER 1
AILA

The narrow alleyway closes in before me, its walls threatening to suffocate me. The path is dimly lit, revealing a landscape of forgotten trash and debris scattered along the ground. My breath comes in short, frantic bursts, each inhale burning my lungs with the scent of fear. The sound of my steps echoes against the brick walls. I hear the sound of his panting breaths, a reminder that he's there, always there, picking up his pace behind me. Suddenly, my foot snags on something unseen, sending me crashing to the ground with a sickening thud.

My hands scrape against the rough asphalt as I scramble to break my fall. Before I can catch my breath, he's towering over me, his figure casting a sinister shadow against the walls. His eyes gleam with appalling hunger. In that moment, as terror grips me, I know that I'm at his mercy.

A twisted grin warps his lips as he brandishes a polished blade. The paces of my heart quicken and I struggle to draw in air. I want to scream, to resist with all my might, or even to let out a faint whisper, pleading for mercy. Fear suppresses my voice, rendering me mute and powerless. My eyes grow as I stare hopelessly in silence.

He's been haunting me for what feels like an eternity and now he's right before me. He kneels beside me, his hot breath brushing against my skin as he leans in to press the cold metal of the knife against my throat.

I squeeze my eyes shut, bracing for the pain to come, the sharp edge of the blade threatening to pierce my skin and spill my blood. A jolt of agony shoots through the nerves of my chin as he applies pressure

Suddenly, I'm jolted awake, my heart hammering against my ribs. Sweat drenches my skin, clinging my shirt to my trembling form. The darkness presses in around me as I strain to make out my surroundings, the familiar contours of my bedroom slowly coming into focus. I'm safe, I remind myself, but the remnants of the nightmare still cling to me.

I try to shake off the fear, to convince myself that it was just a dream, but a dark presence lingers in the corners of my mind, refusing to be banished. I can't help but think that he's still out there, waiting in the shadows for the perfect opportunity to finally finish me.

My gaze flickers to the open doorway, where a dark figure seems to lurk, its shape blending seamlessly with the night. A scream rises in my throat, desperate and primal, tearing through the silence of the room. The sound jolts my husband from his sleep, his eyes wide with alarm as he scrambles to get ahold of me. I cling to him as he holds me tight and close.

"Everything's okay, Aila. It's another nightmare," he says soothingly. He follows my gaze as I point in the direction of the door.

"He's here!" I shout.

He lunges from the bed to flick on the light switch. "It's nothing. No one's there. See?" I let down my head and let out a sigh.

"I'm just hallucinating," I say, the weight of reality settling in. He's right. Another nightmare threatens to consume me, and it doesn't help that, once I wake, it's followed by hallucinations.

But I know these moments all too well. For weeks, my dreams have picked up and become increasingly more terrifying and vivid. An unidentified man hunts me down, threatening to steal the life from me. Each time right before I meet my demise, I am jolted awake. People say dreams like these mean you feel threatened, vulnerable, or are avoiding something. I wish I could buy into that. But my dreams have always been dark. It's ridiculous to think I've been feeling threatened or trying to elude something since I was a kid.

I glance over at the alarm clock - 4:00 am. It means I've only slept for 2 hours. I have no intention of returning to sleep. My husband has already begun to snore again. I slip out of bed and head to the kitchen. On the way, I make sure to flip on every light to brighten my path and reduce surprises. I pour a glass of water and head to the loveseat, which my husband has inadvertently deemed mine due to the amount of time I recently spend in it. I power on the TV, a way to drown out the thoughts festering in my head, and spend the next few hours watching TV into the early morning.

My husband awakens at his usual hour, 6 am sharp. Before he dives into his morning routine, he discovers me nestled in the loveseat, captivated by a true crime series on TV.

"Why do you watch this stuff? I'm sure it's what keeps you up at night," he remarks, planting a tender kiss on my forehead. I choose to brush off his comment, though deep down, I know there might be some truth to it.

"Good morning. Do you have time for breakfast?" I inquire, hoping for a moment of connection before the day sweeps us apart.

"Not today, sorry. You should get some rest." Instead of heeding his advice, I make my way to the kitchen to prepare his lunch and a small on-the-go breakfast. After he showers and dresses, he grabs the meals and heads out for yet another extended day in the office, leaving me alone to wrestle with my thoughts in the quiet emptiness of our home.

There's not much on my agenda for the day. Without kids or even a pet, most of my time is dedicated to myself and my husband. A promotion my husband received a few years back allowed me to resign from work. From the start of our marriage, he insisted I step back from working and focus on my passions. "As long as it's up to me," he'd say, "you should never have to work."

So, usually, I dedicate my time to working out, sewing, and baking. Today, I plan to stop by the gym and also check out the new sports lounge that opened in our neighborhood. I've asked Jaison to make time to try it out with me, but he's been understandably busy with work. In fact, it's been a while since we've been able to get out on the town.

The first years of our marriage, we were inseparable, going out at least twice a week. We tried restaurants, spent evenings in arcades, saw almost every new movie, and took a number of trips. But after five years of marriage, it seems our relationship has been overshadowed by never-ending work shifts.

I quickly shower and dress, pulling my hair back into a messy bun. Opting for comfort, I select a pair of grey leggings, a spaghetti-strapped top in hunter green, and white running sneakers. I tuck my hair through a fitted dad cap before heading out into the morning to start my day.

I spend just an hour in the gym, avoiding the early morning rush of those who sacrifice sleep and mornings to squeeze in a gym session before work. The gym is fairly empty, save for an elderly man taking his time on the treadmill. I gravitate towards the cardio machines and choose the elliptical machine, craving the full-body workout it offers.

With each stride, I feel the tension of the morning loosen its grip on my mind and body. The rhythmic motion of my legs carries me forward, propelling me into a state of focus. As the minutes pass, I gradually increase the intensity, pushing myself to new limits. Beads of sweat form on my brow. With music pouring through my earbuds, I lose myself in the moment.

My attention is immediately captured by the television ahead as the morning news anchor delivers yet another update on the ongoing horror that has gripped our town for months. I remove my earbuds, allowing the anchor's voice to gradually fill the room.

"Good morning, viewers. We bring you a breaking news update from Rutledge, Ohio, where another grisly discovery has shaken the community." Aerial footage shows the suburban neighborhood of Trotter Road, with police vehicles parked outside a residence.

"In the latest development, a body has been found inside a home on Trotter Road, marking the third such incident within a 20-mile radius in recent months. The victim, a man in his mid-40s, was discovered with severe blunt force trauma, suggesting he was beaten with a heavy object." The camera cuts to images of investigators examining the crime scene, with forensic teams collecting evidence.

"Investigators have uncovered a bloody

sledgehammer nearby, leading them to believe it may have been the murder weapon. Disturbingly, there was no sign of forced entry, leaving authorities puzzled as to how the assailant gained access to the home." The camera cuts to the detective addressing reporters at a press conference.

"At this time, the investigation is still ongoing. We are exploring all possible leads and conducting interviews with neighbors and acquaintances of the victim. We urge anyone with information to come forward and assist us in bringing the perpetrator to justice," the detective announces. The camera cuts back to the anchor at the reporting desk.

"As the community grapples with yet another senseless act of violence, residents are urged to remain vigilant and report any suspicious activity to local authorities. We will continue to bring you updates as this story unfolds."

CHAPTER 2
CARTER

I step out of my car and onto the normally quiet street of Trotter Road. Today, it's filled with spectators and reporters lingering, eagerly awaiting updates on the chaos. The flashing lights of the police vehicles illuminate the darkness of the early morning. I've seen my fair share of crime scenes, but each one still manages to send a shudder through me. Approaching the house, I'm met by the somber faces of my fellow officers, their expressions grim as they usher me inside. The scene that unfolds before me is one of utter horror. The victim, a middle-aged man, lies motionless on the floor, his body battered and bruised beyond recognition. I kneel beside him and observe as the man's face is contorted in pain, his features twisted in a silent scream. It's clear he suffered greatly before his death.

"Detective, you need to see this," one of the officers says, gesturing towards a corner of the room. I follow his gaze and my eyes widen at the sight before me. The room is in disarray, furniture overturned and belongings scattered across the floor. It's a scene of disorder, a plain contrast to the quiet suburban neighborhood outside.

My eyes fall upon a weapon lying nearby - a bloodied sledgehammer, its surface stained with the evidence of the violent act that took place here. The sight makes my stomach churn.

"We found this in the backyard," another officer says, handing me a plastic evidence bag containing a piece of torn fabric. I examine it closely and confirm with the officer that it's already been photographed by the forensic photographer. I make quick notes on a small pocket-sized notepad, a habit I formed during my early days on the force.

"It looks like we've got another tough one on our hands," I mutter to myself, knowing that this investigation is far from over.

Back in the office, the burden of the case drapes over me. I feel the weight of expectation from my team, hungry for any shred of progress in our relentless pursuit of answers. The room buzzes with hushed voices, the tension thick enough to slice through. A welcomed aroma greets me as I'm handed a steaming cup of coffee and a flaky Danish by the station's new assistant.

Grateful for the gesture, I nod my thanks and make my way toward the conference room for our afternoon briefing. I take a seat at the head of the table and exhale slowly. Every surface is cluttered with files and evidence.

"Glad to see you're back, Detective Carter," my colleague greets me. "We've been poring over the case."

"What have we uncovered?" I question.

"We've been dissecting the similarities and disparities among the three victims," another detective adds. "It's becoming evident that we may be up against an organized and meticulous killer." As he speaks, I flip through my notepad, absorbing each detail. "For starters, the murder weapons vary drastically. The first victim was drugged and strangled to death, while the second suffered a fatal fall from six stories in his own apartment."

I furrow my brow, grappling with the inconsistencies in the methods of murder. The harsh reality is that these incidents could be entirely unrelated. Yet, Rutledge is known for its tranquility, with the last murder occurring over two decades ago. This leads the department to speculate that there might be a connection. If these crimes were indeed perpetrated by a single suspect, the grim truth emerges: our town may be facing its first serial killer.

Frustration gnaws at me. "There must be some consistencies we can identify," I muse aloud. Detective Booker's voice cuts through the tension like a knife.

"All of the victims are men, but each of different ages."

I lean back in my chair, my fingers threading through my hair as I ponder our next moves. "We need to dig deeper. We have to unearth any connections between the victims, regardless of how insignificant they may seem. That's our best chance at cracking this."

"And what about the media?" another detective interjects, echoing the concerns of the room. "They're itching to know if we're dealing with a potential serial killer."

I cast a glance at the cluttered whiteboard, its surface adorned with photographs and scribbled notes, each one a fragment of the puzzle we're desperately trying to assemble.

"It's too premature to say. If we can unearth a damning connection, only then will we sound the alarm. For now, the town remains vigilant. That's precisely what we need." With that, the meeting draws to a close, and my colleagues disperse to their respective desks and offices.

Back in the relief of my office, my thoughts are consumed by a piece of evidence presented to me earlier. A torn fragment of fabric, its texture suggesting it once belonged to a tan shirt. The evidence is currently undergoing processing, and in a matter of hours or days, we'll receive a comprehensive report detailing its composition. This crucial information will undoubtedly aid us in piecing together the puzzle of how it came to be left behind.

I speculate that during the struggle, the assailant's shirt was torn, inadvertently leaving behind this fragment as they made their escape. If we're fortunate, this piece of cloth could yield DNA evidence, providing us with a significant breakthrough in our investigation.

The remainder of the morning, I'm consumed by the task of unraveling the transcripts from each 911 call reporting the disturbing incidents. What strikes me as peculiar is that all the calls originated from strangers, yet they were made from the victims' own homes. These men were devoid of familial connections or regular check-ins, rendering them vulnerable and solitary. Detective Booker's voice resurfaces in my mind: "The victims are all men." While I brushed aside this observation during the meeting, I find myself unable to shake its significance. Indeed, all of the victims were single men who lived alone. However, the absence of forced entry in any of the incidents adds another layer of perplexity to the puzzle.

Transcript of Call to Emergency Services
Daniel Edwards, Trotter Road

Operator: 911, what's your emergency?
Neighbor: Oh my, oh my! I need help, please!

Operator: Ma'am, please stay calm. What's happening?

Neighbor: I... I think my neighbor is dead! There's blood everywhere, and he's not moving!

Operator: Okay, ma'am, I need you to tell me where you are so we can send help right away.

Neighbor: My address is 1210 Trotter Rd. I am at my neighbor's. The address... I can get you his address. It's 1212. 1212 Trotter- Please help!

Operator: Help is on the way, ma'am. Can you tell me if you saw anyone come or go from the house?

Neighbor: No, I haven't seen anyone! I just heard a ruckus. I looked from my window and couldn't see much. I went up to my room to dress myself. When I came over to check, the door was unlocked, and... and I found him!

Operator: Alright, ma'am, try to stay calm. Don't touch anything, and wait for the emergency services to arrive. They'll take care of everything.

Neighbor: Okay, okay. Please, hurry!

Operator: They're on their way. Just stay on the line with me until they get there. Can you tell me if you see anyone else around the area?

Neighbor: No, I don't see anyone. It's just me.

Operator: Alright, thank you for the information, ma'am. Help is coming. Just hold on.

Neighbor: Okay, thank you!

**Transcript of Call to Emergency Services
Liam Harris, Main Street & Elm Ave**

Operator: 911, what's your emergency?

Caller: Oh God, please, send help! I-I was walking down the street, and this man just... he fell from the building!

Operator: Okay, sir, I need you to take a deep breath and tell me where you are.

Caller: I'm going to vomit. Oh God!

Operator: Sir, please remain calm. Can you tell me your location?

Caller: I'm on Main Street, near the intersection with Elm Avenue.

Operator: Alright, sir. Did you see anyone else around the area?

Caller: No, no, it happened so fast! I ran to him, but... but he was already... he was already on the ground.

Operator: Okay, sir. Did you notice anything unusual before the fall?

Caller: No, nothing! It was quiet, and then... and then he fell! I-I started shouting for help, but... but I don't know if anyone saw anything.

Operator: Alright, sir. Help is on the way. Stay where you are and try to keep calm.

Transcript of Call to Emergency Services
Jacob Garcia, Marginal Trail

Operator: 911, what's your emergency?

Cleaner: Hola, yes, uh... help, please!

Operator: Okay, what's the emergency?

Cleaner: Um, we, uh... came to clean house, but... um, man... in bed, no move.

Operator: Alright, sir, can you tell me the address of the house you're at?

Cleaner: Uh, sí, sí, is 741 Marginal Trail.

Operator: Help is on the way, sir. Is the man breathing? Is he conscious?

Cleaner: No, no move. No se mueve. Only in underpants.

Operator: Okay, sir. Do you see anyone else around? Is anyone else in the house?

Cleaner: No, solo nosotros. No comprendemos.

Operator: Alright, sir. The paramedics are on their way. Don't touch anything and wait for them to arrive. Make sure to stay safe.

Cleaner: Gracias, thank you! Por favor, rápido!

Operator: They're on their way, sir. Just hold on. Thank you for calling 911.

A knock on my office door interrupts my concentration. "It's Harper," the familiar voice announces. Harper, the precinct's new administrative assistant, hired to manage clerical tasks, schedule appointments, and generate reports among other duties. However, her tendency to blur the lines between professional and personal support is evident. Despite my reassurances that she needn't bring coffee or order lunch, she persists.

A week ago, she surprised me with a Philly cheesesteak from my favorite sub spot, and I promised to repay her. Glancing at my watch, I realize it's nearing lunchtime on the day I vowed to treat her. "Come in," I call out, and the door creaks open as she enters.

"Hey, are you ready?" she asks eagerly.

"Just about," I respond, swiftly gathering and stowing away the scattered documents. With my jacket and keys in hand, we set out together.

CHAPTER 3
AILA

I weave through the busy streets of downtown Rutledge making my way towards the new sports lounge on foot. It's a fair distance from our modest apartment. As I step inside, the ambiance immediately fascinates me. The décor is modern and updated, with clean lines and minimalist furnishings that create an inviting atmosphere. Soft lighting casts a gentle glow over the full bar, showcasing an enticing array of drinks.

The lounge area is spacious and relaxing, with various seating options for socializing. Bowling lanes stretch along one side while dartboards line the other. In a cozy corner, secluded hookah booths line the walls. The air is laced with the sweet scent of flavored tobacco. The vibe is laid-back and inviting.

I slip into a booth tucked away in a far corner of the sports lounge. I take a moment to examine the menu provided via a QR code affixed to the table. Surprisingly, twenty minutes pass without any sign of a waiter. Glancing around the sparsely populated eating area, I notice the scattered presence of patrons engrossed in various activities. Spotting only a lone bartender behind the bar, I make my way over to him, politely voicing my concern about the lack of service at my table.

He chuckles in response, causing me to momentarily question if my complaint came across as humorous. However, as I meet his eyes with a stern look, his smile fades, and he explains the lounge's unique approach.

"Our lounge doesn't offer traditional waiter service," he clarifies. "Instead, you can use the QR code to browse the menu and place your order directly from your phone."

"And what if I don't have a phone?"

"You're welcome to order directly from the bar," he replies.

"Oh," I mutter, abruptly ending the conversation before retreating to my seat. I take a moment to order garlic parmesan wings, fries, and a Coke, then fish my phone out of my handbag. I prefer to lurk in the shadows of the online world. My social media profile remains dormant, devoid of updates about my thoughts or activities. I don't bother with selfies or sharing details about my appearance. When it comes to connecting with others, I favor more traditional methods: phone calls, texts, and face-to-face meetings.

Still, I maintain a social media presence to stay informed about what others are up to, local and world news, and current trends. From the corner of my eye, I notice the bartender's gaze lingering on me. Shrugging off the scrutiny, I dive into my wings. At the bar, there's a woman patiently waiting for service. The bartender takes a moment to attend to her, their conversation too distant for me to hear. However, the look on his face suggests he's preoccupied. I steal a few glances and realize he's uncomfortably focused on me. A pang of unease settles in as I wonder if my earlier sharp response has upset him.

As I finish the last bite of my food, I linger at the table, pretending to be engrossed in my phone. Part of me yearns to prove the bartender's watchful gaze, while another half debates whether to confront him directly. But the fear of the unknown holds me back—I can't be certain of anyone's true intentions.

When I glance over and catch him scowling, I decide to hold his gaze, unflinchingly meeting his stare. It's a silent acknowledgment that I'm aware of his scrutiny. Before I know it, my feet carry me to the bar, my purse and phone clutched tightly in my hand.

"Is there a problem?" I ask firmly, my voice betraying a hint of apprehension. His brows furrow in confusion as he takes a step back.

"What do you mean?" he responds.

"I've noticed you glancing in my direction all afternoon. It's making me uncomfortable." He raises his hands in a gesture of defense.

"I'm sorry, ma'am. I'm not sure what you're talking about. I may have glanced over once or twice, but it's my job to keep an eye on the patrons. Since we don't have traditional waiters, I need to notify the staff when it seems like customers are finishing up their meals. And, of course, I wanted to ensure you were taken care of."

I reluctantly accept his explanation, though skepticism gnaws at the edges of my mind. Deep down, I know that pressing the issue further won't lead to any resolution.

"Sure thing," I reply before slipping out. I manage to make it home before Jaison arrives. Settling into my spot on the loveseat, I find myself succumbing to the sleep I've been evading. I struggle to keep my eyes open, fighting against the urge to let them shut. As I lie back, covered in a throw blanket, my mind drifts off. I suddenly become aware of a heavy weight pressing down on my chest. Dread rushes through me as I try to move, but my body feels like it's encased in lead, immobile and unresponsive.

I attempt to call out, hoping a neighbor can hear my screams through the thin walls, but no sound escapes my lips. The room is bathed in an eerie half-light, shadows dancing ominously along the walls. I feel a presence looming over me, unseen but intense, filling me with anxiety. My heart races, pounding in my ears as I struggle against the invisible force pinning me down.

I try to rationalize, telling myself it's just a dream, but the sensation is all too real. Time seems to stretch on endlessly as I battle against the paralysis, each second feeling like an eternity. Desperate for release, I focus all my energy on moving a single finger, a tiny gesture of defiance against the suffocating grip of sleep paralysis.

Finally, I manage to break free from the invisible shackles holding me captive. Gasping for air, I sit up on the loveseat as I try to shake off the lingering feeling of unease. The room returns to normal. It's silent and still. As exhaustion envelops me once more, I surrender and drift off into a peaceful slumber.

When I awake in the evening, I find myself still on the loveseat, cocooned beneath a thicker blanket. My husband has returned and instead of stirring me from my sleep, he has chosen to let me rest, retreating to our bed alone. It's too late now to disturb him for the engagement I had been longing for. I wish he had woken me upon his arrival, but the opportunity has slipped away. Climbing into bed, I find myself wide awake, the burst of energy from my extended nap coursing through me.

Thoughts whirl through my mind and my attention is drawn to the unfortunate news that another murder has shaken our town— the third in just two months. The first two had sent shockwaves through the community, as our city had been relatively free of violent crime, with incidents mostly limited to theft and vandalism.

It all began with the grisly discovery of a man strangled to death in his own home, the toxicology reports revealing traces of drugs in his system. Initially, investigators suspected a personal motive, but as their inquiries yielded no evidence to support this theory, the case grew increasingly confusing.

Jacob Garcia was a figure of success, portrayed by the internet as a loving and accomplished self-employed realtor. His online profiles painted a picture of a man deeply passionate about real estate and entrepreneurship— a self-made guru in his field. The revelation of his untimely demise sent shockwaves rippling through the community. It was his cleaning staff who made the grim discovery, stumbling upon his lifeless body within the confines of his own home.

Liam Harris, on the other hand, remained largely invisible in the digital realm. Descriptions of him in news articles painted a different picture—a man residing in a neighborhood plagued by violence, working at a local food plant. His online presence was minimal, if nonexistent, leaving little trace of his life for the world to see. Even his ex-wife, with whom he shared children, remained elusive, unreachable by the probing questions of the media.

The circumstances surrounding Liam's death were equally unsettling. Initially dismissed as a tragic accident—a fall from his apartment balcony—it soon became apparent that there was more to the story. Evidence pointed to foul play, suggesting Liam had been enjoying a quiet moment on his balcony, savoring a beer, before being approached from behind and violently pushed to his death.

With Liam's demise following closely on the heels of Jacob Garcia's murder, the town was thrown into a frenzy of fear and speculation. Two seemingly unconnected deaths, both shrouded in mystery and tragedy, were enough to ignite an uproar.

The thought of a lurking predator prowling the streets of our town worries at me, amplifying the restlessness that already plagues my nights. The police struggle to unearth a lead and it's become increasingly evident that they're grasping at straws. Daniel Edwards, the latest casualty, met a grisly fate within the confines of his own home—brutally bludgeoned to death. The details remain scant. I turn to the internet, searching online platforms for updates and clues. Among them, a neighbor's hesitance to alert authorities at the first sign of trouble has become a focal point of scrutiny. Users ponder why she didn't immediately contact the police.

The constant stream of worrying thoughts swirls around in my mind, keeping me on edge. I can't shake the feeling of unease, wondering who might be the next target and if my loved ones are safe. Since I started following the news about these murders, sleep has become a rare commodity. Tonight, I lie in bed staring at the ceiling, feeling the weight of the darkness pressing down on me. Sleep seems like a distant dream, slipping further away with each passing minute. It's just another night of restless tossing and turning, haunted by what's unfolding.

CHAPTER 4
CARTER

The analysis of the torn cloth yields disappointing results: it's just a piece from a hand cloth, likely used for yard work, and DNA evidence suggests it belonged to the victim. Another dead end for us. With the recent escalation in murders, we're under pressure to solve these cases, and fast. Our next lead is speaking with Ms. Mary Byrne, the neighbor who made the initial 911 call for Daniel Edwards. She might have valuable information. Despite her protests to stay together, I've assigned Detective Booker to look into Jacob Garcia's building for any security breaches. We need to cover all bases in a short time. As for me, I'll handle Ms. Byrne alone.

Arriving at Ms. Byrne's house, I notice how close it is to the victim's home. With the curtains drawn back, it's easy to see into each other's lives. Their houses are separated only by a driveway and a sliver of grass. Glancing around the neighborhood, it seems tranquil. Despite it being a weekday afternoon, the driveways are packed with cars, hinting that most of the neighbors are home, perhaps retirees. The well-maintained yards and absence of clutter suggest a community of homeowners, not families with children. It's a telling sight; people who care for their homes often reflect a certain stability.

Ms. Byrne is quick to answer the door, greeting me with a warm smile. "Ms. Byrne," I say, extending my hand for a shake.

"Detective Carter. Come right in," she replies, her hands enveloping mine with a reassuring warmth. As I enter, the soothing scent of mint tea fills the air, mingling with the soft murmur of the television. The anchor's voice drifts through the room, narrating local news stories. While the house is tidy and well-organized, the furniture feels a touch outdated. Ms. Byrnes, a woman in her late 50s, lives alone in this widowed state.

She gestures for me to take a seat on the living room sofa as she heads to the kitchen, offering tea. I decline, keeping my focus on the matter at hand. Sheer ivory curtains adorn the large windows, offering privacy from the outside world. Yet, from within, it seems as though anyone could peer in. The view from the side window only reveals shrubs and glimpses of Daniel Edward's home. Not much of a vantage point. Perhaps there's another window downstairs from which she could have observed after hearing the commotion.

Returning to the living room, she settles into an armchair across from me. "Ms. Byrnes, as you know—" I begin, but she interrupts, correcting me.

"Mrs. Byrnes," she says firmly.

"My apologies, Mrs. Byrnes. I wanted to meet with you to perhaps delve into more detail about what you saw on the morning you discovered Mr. Edwards."

"Yes, of course."

"If you don't mind briefly recalling your account of the events, please."

"Well, it was late in the evening. Well, technically

the morning. I'd woken up to use the restroom and grab a glass of water. I heard maybe a scream come from over there. I thought maybe it was my mind playing tricks because of the sleepiness. I hadn't thought much of it. I used the restroom and went to lie down, and then I thought I heard a crash. I took a peek through the curtains down here, and I mean, I could see the street and house, nothing was going on out there. I didn't have much on, so I went to change from my gown, and that's when I went over and discovered him," she explains.

"About what time did you hear what you thought was a scream?"

"I'm not sure. It was late. Definitely after midnight because I went to bed just before midnight and had been sleeping."

"Today you said when you heard the noise, you went to lie down again. Before, you said you changed and went right over."

"Well, I didn't think much of the scream. People scream for many reasons. I stub a toe and I'll let out a screech. So, when I called the police, I was explaining from the time I heard the loud crash," she clarifies.

I nod in understanding. "How much time would you say lapsed between the scream and crash?"

"I don't know. You just don't think to track things like that in the heat of the moment. It was late. It couldn't be long."

"When you looked out the window, what did you see?"

"I told you guys. Nothing. The road was just as empty as always."

"And what about your relationship with your neighbor, Mr. Edwards?" I inquire.

She hesitates, her finger tapping nervously against her leg. "Well, um, I don't really know him well. He was strange and kept to himself mostly," she stammers.

"What do you mean by strange?"

"He wasn't much of a community person. You know, this neighborhood, we're tight-knit. But he never participated in any gatherings or events. Hardly ever said a word when we passed each other. Seemed like he preferred his own company. Can't say I blame him. People around here didn't exactly warm up to him. He was an outsider. I wasn't exactly thrilled about him myself," she confesses, then halts abruptly. "Sorry, I shouldn't have said that. May he rest in peace. But yeah, he was just... different."

I jot down notes, processing her words. "Did anyone in the neighborhood express animosity towards Mr. Edwards more openly?"

She shakes her head. "Not really. We're an older bunch here. We got the message. No one bothered to hassle him."

Closing my notepad, I slide it back into my pocket. "That's all for now, Mrs. Byrne. Thanks for your time," I say, preparing to leave.

"Are you sure?" she asks. I nod.

"Mind if I ask you something?" she adds. I nod again.

"The city's buzzing about a serial killer. What if he strikes again close by?"

"We're not jumping to conclusions just yet. The evidence doesn't point to a single perpetrator. But we're investigating thoroughly. Rest assured, we're doing everything we can to keep the community safe."

She sighs, unconvinced. "Hope you're right. I just hope you guys have this all under control before he strikes again. Thanks for listening," she says as I make my way to the door.

"Thank you again for your time."

CHAPTER 5
AILA

Jaison and I had a dispute this morning before he headed out. He thinks I should leave the investigation of the recent murders to the police and move on. When I mentioned the wealth of information I found online, he urged me to stop digging into it, worried about my well-being. I reassured him that I'm fine and reminded him that my sleeping issues come and go. Restlessness has been a part of my life since childhood, sometimes accompanied by nightmares, hallucinations, and even sleep paralysis. I've learned that changes in circumstances or stress levels can trigger it, which is why I'm determined to assist the police department in any way I can.

Jaison won't admit it, but I believe he's concerned about me getting too wrapped up in work again. I was once a records specialist at the Rutledge Police Department. I was a diligent police records clerk, valued by the team for my meticulous attention to detail and efficiency. However, whispers began circulating among the department's staff about my prolonged stays on the department's computer system, often lingering long after my scheduled shift had ended. Initially dismissed as dedication, concerns arose when it became clear that my late-night sessions were unrelated to my assigned duties.

Rumors grew, suggesting that I was accessing files beyond my responsibilities. Raised eyebrows and uneasy glances followed me around the office for weeks. The situation reached a climax when the IT security team discovered unauthorized access to restricted files, all linked to my user account. Investigation revealed that I had been delving into closed investigations, examining case notes and evidence logs without proper authorization.

I denied any wrongdoing at first, insisting that I was merely researching to better understand department operations. But under mounting pressure, I reluctantly confessed to the unauthorized access.

Dismissal seemed imminent, but I had allies who intervened on my behalf. Instead, I faced suspension without pay and mandatory retraining on data security and ethical conduct protocols. When Jaison learned of this, I confessed my fascination with criminal cases studied up close.

In college, I studied office management, which led me to an administrative role. However, a passion for investigating and analyzing crimes soon rose. I toyed with the idea of returning to school to pursue criminology, but that dream died when I made the decision to resign from the department and stay home instead. Jaison believed it was the best course of action, fearing I might dig myself into a legal hole. The department had let me off with a mere slap on the wrist, but it could have been much worse. The recent string of crimes has reignited my passion for investigation.

Without informing Jaison, I set out on a mission to Trotter Rd, intent on surveilling Daniel Edwards' neighbors and his residence. I take the light rail transit to the neighborhood, where I begin my journey on foot, carefully scrutinizing each address until I spot the house mentioned in the reports. However, upon arrival, I find the area crowded with police personnel, making my task more challenging. I pull my hoodie lower over my head to remain discreet.

As I scan the surroundings, I lock eyes with a neighbor peering nervously from her window. The abrupt closure of her curtains suggests she's cautious of prying eyes. I make a beeline for her door, navigating my way to avoid any surveillance cameras or curious onlookers.

When I knock, she cautiously cracks the door, her gaze suspicious and guarded. "I've made it clear to your team and others—I won't speak to the media," she asserts firmly.

"I'm not here representing the media. I reside just around the corner, a block away," I lie. "I'm concerned for our community's safety. Relying solely on law enforcement may not suffice." Just as she moves to shut the door, I interject, subtly blocking its closure with my foot. "I'm an independent investigator. I believe there's a serial killer on the loose. He's already struck close to our neighborhood, and I fear..." As I'm about to finish my plea, the door abruptly shuts in my face. I turn to leave when the unmistakable sound of chains being removed freezes me in place. Without hesitation, she swings the door wide open, gesturing urgently for me to step inside.

Mary introduces herself as we enter the living room, her face familiar from the news reports detailing the discovery of Daniel Edwards' body. She gestures toward the sofa, indicating I should take a seat. I explain that I've been delving into the cases, attempting to unravel the mystery.

"I'm sorry to hear about the online scrutiny you've

faced," I offer sympathetically. The internet hasn't been kind to Mary since her televised account. Many speculate that living so close, she must have witnessed more than she let on.

"It's okay. I don't spend any time online, so I won't see any of it."

"They think you're a suspect," I blurt out, my words catching her off guard. Her eyes widen, a hand instinctively moving to her chest.

"A suspect? That's absurd!"

"But considering the circumstances of his death, he must have been attacked before you found him," I remark, more as a statement than a question.

"That's correct," she confirms.

"Well, that means you missed the killer by a long shot. I don't believe you saw anything."

"I didn't," she insists.

"What that means is, if you heard a commotion and rushed over after getting dressed, you'd likely have encountered the killer. Yet, you only arrived after he'd been beaten to death and the killer managed to escape. It's possible it happened within such a short window, but that seems unlikely," I explain. Mary stares at me, seemingly lost in thought.

"Who did you say you were again?" she asks, her voice tinged with suspicion.

"My name is Katy Brown," I reply, maintaining my cover.

"You're with the police, aren't you? I'm going to be arrested," she says, fear evident in her shaky voice.

"Why would you be arrested? What else do you know, Mary?" I press.

Her demeanor shifts, a sense of apprehension

creeping into her voice. "I... I didn't tell the whole truth. I heard a commotion, a shout, but I didn't know Daniel well. I didn't think much of it. People argue for various reasons. I locked my doors and went back to bed, shortly after midnight. When I woke in the morning, his car hadn't moved, which was unusual. I figured that maybe he took the public transit into the city. Something urged me to check. I've checked around before while he was away when the rest of the community just didn't trust him. When I peeked through the window, I saw what I thought was him lying there, maybe unconscious from a fall. That's when I went in."

"And the door was open?"

"It was closed but unlocked. It's not an unusual occurrence around here. The neighborhood is extremely safe... well, it was. Plenty of people keep their doors unlocked."

"I see," I nod, taking in her explanation.

"And so, you can understand why I felt so bad that I couldn't admit the truth. I am struggling to get past this mistake. I've been watching investigators come and go and can only think about if I had the chance to save the man and ignored it. If you have to take me in, I understand."

My brows furrow at her statement. "Mary, I'm not a cop. I'm dressed in a hoodie, cap, and sweatpants. I'm just like you—shaken and confused. This isn't your fault. You probably saved your own life by not intervening. I think if you are starting to feel too guilty, you should maybe just update the police with the true version of the events before they discover it themselves and turn their attention to you."

Mary's head droops as she refuses to make eye contact, but she agrees. "Will you keep in touch?" she asks.

"I'll take down your contact details and as I come

across more details, I will update you," I promise.

She nods and offers a slight smile before showing me out the door. I take a look around the street, and it seems the other neighbors have no desire to be involved, as none are lurking about. As I check my phone, I feel a buzz, and it's a message from Jaison.

See you soon.

I panic briefly. I forgot that Jaison and I agreed to meet for lunch, a thing we hadn't done in so long. I'm on the other side of town, getting around by public transit. It'd be an hour before I made it back to our side of town and another hour to change and meet him at the agreed-upon diner. Lunch is in 20 minutes. I regretfully send a text message asking to take a rain check.

During my lengthy commute back to my apartment, I finally act on a thought that's been brewing in my mind. I create a new social media page on Echo titled **Shadow Stalker Updates**. It's evident that there's a dangerous individual on the loose, and I feel compelled to keep my community informed about what the police department might be concealing. I'll share updates from the media and any information I gather from witnesses, making sure to clearly label anything unverified by the authorities. I've decided to dub the culprit "Shadow Stalker," the figure haunting my dreams and robbing me of sleep. My goal is to rally the community together and bring this killer to justice before they strike again.

CHAPTER 6
CARTER

I arrive at the precinct early, eager to review the evidence collected from the recent crime scenes. Harper, always thoughtful, brings me coffee shortly after my arrival. I express my gratitude and she places the coffee on my desk, lingering for a moment as I sift through the files. I glance up from my work, peering over the rim of my glasses. "Need something?" I inquire.

She hesitates for a moment before deciding against whatever is on her mind and turns to leave. I halt her departure, encouraging her to speak her mind. "It's just... whenever I bring you coffee, or anything really, I've noticed you never actually partake in it. I'm trying to understand you," she confesses. I hadn't realized she had been paying attention. No one else ever has, outside of my wife. She's perceptive.

I've had my fair share of challenges in life, and one of them has left me wary of consuming food or drinks that I haven't prepared or witnessed being prepared. It's a source of tension with my wife, who yearns to know more about my past. I've told her I was adopted and she assumes my reserve about my childhood stems from that. She enjoys dining out, but I'm always hesitant due to my lingering distrust.

Nevertheless, I've never found myself in a position where I needed to explain my peculiar behavior in detail. "I've mentioned before that bringing me food and coffee isn't necessary. There are certain food items I simply don't partake in," I explain.

"Well, if coffee isn't your thing, what else could I bring? I distinctly recall our conversation about Philly steaks, but now that I think about it, when I brought it in, I hadn't seen you indulge in that either," she remarks. I realize that Harper is genuinely interested, and I can't risk complicating matters by concealing the truth.

"Harper, I have a habit of being cautious about consuming anything I haven't personally seen prepared. It may seem odd, but it's just how I operate. It's nothing personal."

"Interesting," she murmurs, clearly intrigued by my explanation.

"I've witnessed my fair share of unsettling situations over the years. It's a reality I can't seem to shake."

"I understand."

She works her way around my desk to recover the coffee she'd sat down. She isn't careful to not brush her knee against my leg, contact that sends a wave of discomfort through me. I instinctively lean back in my chair, allowing her to reach for the cup without further contact.

"Excuse me," she apologizes, noting the surprise in my expression. "I just couldn't bear to see it go to waste." She takes a sip of the coffee, maintaining unbroken eye contact, almost as if she's sending a message. "Perhaps one day you'll let me showcase my culinary skills, and I can whip up a meal for us," she suggests.

I swallow nervously, feeling the discomfort escalate. My palms grow clammy as I brush them against my slacks. My gaze drifts to the heart-shaped frame on my desk, enclosing a cherished photo. Following my gaze, she notices the photo and blushes deeply, hastily gulping down more coffee in embarrassment.

Quickly backtracking, she adds, "Oh, I mean as colleagues. We could invite Booker and the others along too."

Finally finding my voice, I say, "We should talk. Please, take a seat," gesturing towards the chair across from my desk. "I want to make it clear that as a professional team, we need to establish clear boundaries," I start, my tone assertive yet measured. "I appreciate your contributions to the precinct, and I'm pleased to have you on board. However, I've noticed some behavior that crosses the line of appropriateness. While I'm fine with occasional social interactions, recent incidents have raised concerns."

I pause, observing her reaction as I continue, "During lunch the other day, I observed behavior that was overly friendly, and today, it seems to have repeated. Consider this a warning to dial it back. We need to ensure our actions don't lead to unintended consequences. I trust you understand the seriousness of the matter."

I catch her stealing another glance at the photo on my desk — a cherished image of Phoebe, my wife. It's a candid moment frozen in time, captured during a peaceful afternoon picnic in the park. Phoebe sits gracefully, her gaze fixed on the distant lake, while a gentle breeze tousles her honey-blonde hair. I remember the warmth of that moment, the laughter shared as we fed the birds. The memory brings a sweet twinge to my heart, a reminder of the life waiting for me beyond the precinct walls.

"Is that your wife?" Harper asks, trying to shift the conversation. I nod. "She's beautiful. Look, I sincerely apologize if my behavior has made you uncomfortable. We were all pretty close at the law firm where I worked before, but I understand that it might not translate well here. Your concerns are noted, and I'll make sure to be more mindful in the future."

"Did you need anything else?"

"No, I have what I need. Thank you," she responds before exiting the room.

As Harper leaves, Booker sticks her head between the open door. I gesture for her to enter. "Detective, any updates after meeting with Mrs. Byrnes?" she inquires.

"Not much. She's still shaken up and doesn't seem to know anything beyond what was reported in the news. I think we should give her some space unless new leads point back in her direction."

"What about the gap in time?" Booker probes, her brow furrowing with concern.

"She mentioned it was late, and she lost track of time. My guess is she didn't hear anything until it was too late to intervene."

Booker nods thoughtfully. "Okay, Liam Harris' building has cameras. I think we should get a subpoena and take a look. The owner wasn't present, and no one in the neighborhood is willing to talk to the police. I'm sure the cameras captured something," she suggests.

"On it," I respond as she turns to exit.

I'm one step ahead of Booker. I know about the cameras and have already devised a plan to handle them. On my way home, I make a detour to a small house on Journey Lane. It's a nondescript single-floor ranch, but it's serving as an office. I park my car a block away to avoid detection, and I disguise myself with a brimmed hat and a neck scarf pulled up to my nose. It's an unusually warm day for such attire, but it's necessary to avoid unwanted attention.

Approaching the ranch on foot, I tread carefully up the dirt driveway, my hand resting on my gun in its holster. I can't afford to let my guard down; I don't know what to expect. As instructed, I head to the rear of the building, where I find a drop box connecting the exterior to the office inside. I deposit an envelope containing a check into the slot.

Suddenly, I notice a subtle movement behind the curtains, indicating that someone is watching me. My instincts kick in, and I tilt my head slightly, scanning the surroundings for any signs of danger. I stride quickly back down the block to my vehicle, turning around a few times to check for any potential followers. I let out a sigh of relief as I make it back to my parked vehicle and confirm that I haven't been trailed.

As soon as I step foot into our home, my wife greets me from the living room. The familiar aroma of garlic and onions wafts through the air, signaling that she's prepared dinner. I pull her into a warm embrace, as she plants a gentle kiss on my lips.

"What's with the scarf and jacket? Did you not check the weather?" she asks, a hint of amusement in her voice.

"I'm afraid not," I say with a chuckle. "I was sure it was going to rain again, and the scarf... I don't know, the temps were lower in the early morning."

She smiles, her eyes crinkling at the corners. "I've got something for you," she announces, disappearing into the back room. Moments later, she returns with a large canvas in hand. With a flourish, she flips it to reveal a painting—a colorful portrait of me as a teenager, with a woman standing behind me, her hands gently resting on my shoulders. I'm depicted sitting in a chair, a broad smile adorning my youthful face.

I stare at the painting in surprise, marveling at the vibrant colors and uncanny details. My wife has captured my teenage self with remarkable accuracy, drawing inspiration from the few photos I've allowed her to see. But it's the woman standing behind me that perplexes me. With her chestnut skin and a full head of chocolate brown locs, her features mirror mine in an almost eerie manner.

"It's your mom," she says. "Well, at least how I imagine her to look."

I can't help but let out a chuckle, knowing she's way off the mark. My mom, with her mocha brown skin and her signature finger waves bleached to a contrasting blonde, looked nothing like the woman depicted in the painting. But I decide to let it slide. Correcting her would only lead to a tedious conversation about my family history, something I'd rather avoid.

Instead, I offer a grateful smile and say, "It's beautiful." She moves the painting to a corner near our patio, where it joins a collection of other pieces scattered around the room. Phoebe has always been an impeccable painter, her talent evident since childhood. While she's sold a few designs to family and friends, I can't help but think that if she had pursued painting professionally, she'd have her own successful gallery by now. She insists it's not her calling.

We spend the evening discussing updates on the cases I'm working, savoring the bacon cheeseburgers she prepared as we relax on the sofa. I've shielded my wife from many of the grim details, not wanting to add to her fears. The town is gripped by paranoia, convinced that a cunning killer is prowling the streets, and trust in the police force is dwindling. As the leader of the task force, the burden weighs heavily on my shoulders. I can't bear to see my wife fretting over my safety as I pursue an elusive and dangerous individual.

CHAPTER 7
AILA

Liam resided at the notorious intersection of Main and Elm Street, an area bursting with life, especially after dark. Positioned squarely in Rutledge's gritty heart, it's a neighborhood where people wander about into the wee hours. Despite the constant activity, the silence surrounding Liam's murder is deafening. In a neighborhood accustomed to violence, residents have mastered the art of turning a blind eye to the darker deeds that unfold.

Even with a murder in their backyard, the community remains tight-lipped. The streets may buzz with whispered rumors, but when it comes to talking to the authorities, lips are sealed. If the locals won't open up to the police, perhaps they'll be more forthcoming with someone who's just a community member.

I avoid my usual branded attire, opting instead for casual clothing that blends seamlessly with the urban backdrop. The buildings are adorned with layers of graffiti, a testament to their neglect. The entrance facing Main Street appears inaccessible, so I pivot towards a side entrance, hoping for better luck. Like the front entrance, this one is equipped with a buzzing system, a security measure common in these parts. I weigh my options, considering waiting for a resident to come or go, but time is not on my side. With seconds ticking away, I decide to take a gamble and punch in random codes, hoping to strike gold.

After several failed attempts, the fourth apartment finally responds. A woman's voice crackles through the speaker, catching me off guard. "Who's there?" she demands. My mind races, scrambling for a response, but before I can gather my thoughts, she abruptly cuts the connection.

I scan my surroundings, noticing a security camera fixed at the entrance, capturing my every move. With a sinking feeling, I reach for the door, fully expecting it to remain locked. To my surprise, it swings open. It dawns on me that the buzzing system is out of order, explaining why most of my attempts went unnoticed. The building, it seems, allows easy access.

In the main hall, another camera glares with a solid green light, a silent sentinel overseeing the building's activities. I circle the interior, noting cameras stationed at every entry and exit. Despite the building's shabby appearance, its security appears fair aside from the broken doors. With the elevator out of order and Liam's apartment on the sixth floor, I brace myself for the climb. News reports claim he fell from the sixth story, so I ascend six flights of stairs, each step a reminder of the urgency of my mission.

Arriving at the designated floor, I scan the hallway, with my senses on high alert. Liam's apartment should be on the left, toward the end of the corridor. I remain vigilant for any signs of danger. Picking the lock proves to be a simple task; the old-fashioned device yields easily to my expertise. With the door unlocked, I slip inside and quietly close it behind me, shrouding myself in darkness.

My eyes strain in the dimness, prompting me to retrieve my phone and activate its flashlight. The beam pierces the gloom, revealing the vague outlines of objects in the room. Stepping cautiously forward, I enter what appears to be the living area, with the kitchen to my left, separated by a worn countertop. On my right, another room awaits, its floor strewn with scattered debris. Time is of the essence, urging me to swiftly scour the area for any clues.

I'm particularly eager to examine the balcony, but stepping outside poses a risk of being spotted. An unwelcome intruder in the apartment of a deceased individual is sure to make news headlines and land me in a legal battle. From a shadowy corner, I peer through the double sliding doors, veiled by a delicate sheer curtain. Outside, a lone chair sits ominously.

Contemplating the scene, I wonder if someone could have approached Liam from behind, catching him off guard, particularly if he was intoxicated. But what could have motivated such a sudden, violent act? The apartment remains undisturbed, frozen in time since law enforcement conducted their initial assessment. It's clear that the owner has refrained from tampering with the scene, either out of respect or at the request of the authorities.

Despite the likelihood that the police have meticulously combed through every inch of this space, my determination to uncover the truth remains. I spend a few moments sifting through the debris, searching for any clue, yet the scattered remnants offer nothing out of the ordinary, leaving me feeling disheartened. I decide to canvass the building once more, knocking on each door of the sixth floor.

Undoubtedly I receive no response—a blatant reminder of the silent nature of this neighborhood. As I reach the end of the hallway, I reluctantly accept defeat. My efforts have yielded little progress, and I contemplate calling it a night. The thought occurs to me that the police must possess valuable information regarding potential suspects, especially considering the surveillance cameras installed throughout the building. Though, the cameras fail to cover the entrances to individual apartments.

Returning to the first landing, I spot a woman huddled in a corner, cocooned beneath a few worn blankets. Her disheveled appearance catches my attention, and I approach her cautiously, offering a small token of goodwill in the form of a twenty-dollar bill. Her eyes light up with gratitude as she accepts the money, but her response to my inquiry is curt and guarded.

"Do you live here?" I ask, hoping to collect any insight into the residents of this building. Yet, her annoyance is noticeable as she deflects my question, expressing her desire for solitude. Undeterred, I reveal my true purpose, explaining that I am a private investigator hired to ensure the safety of the community—a role that necessitates thorough inquiry and diligence. Her mention of a certain Lewis piques my interest, and I press for more information.

"Who hired you, Lewis?" she retorts bitterly, revealing her strained relationship with the building's landlord. Her words paint a grim picture of neglect and exploitation, hinting at a deeper layer of corruption. "I'm just trying to get a little rest, and then I'll be on my way."

"I'm not here to stop you," I assure her, hoping to ease her apprehension. "We want to prevent any further incidents like the one that occurred here a few weeks ago."

"Lewis went spending money on an irrelevant cop instead of keeping up with this building. He isn't my landlord anymore, but he's shady. He threw me out without giving me a chance. Just a money-hungry slumlord, that's what he is."

"I'm sorry to hear that. Do you need food? Maybe we could grab a burger down the block and chat," I propose.

"I ain't got nothing to talk about with the police."

"I'm not with the department. I'd be bringing you in for trespassing." She responds with a skeptical eye roll.

"Well, I'm not hungry anyway," she dismisses, withdrawing further into her blankets.

"Ma'am, Liam was killed by a serial killer. It might not be safe for you to sleep out here. I'd consider finding a shelter."

"The police claim there's no serial killer on the loose. Liam probably got mixed up with the wrong crowd, and it caught up with him. He spent most of his days drinking himself unconscious anyway. He was miserable. Maybe someone did him a favor. We all thought he jumped," she reveals bitterly.

The words echo in my mind, haunting me with doubt. Did the police make a mistake? Surely, they must have someone captured on camera entering and exiting the building that day, which is why they labeled it as a murder. But how could the residents who knew Liam see it differently? Perplexed, I realize why Liam couldn't defend himself. He never saw it coming.

Before I head home, I take a moment to update my followers. Since creating the page, I've only gathered 12 followers, likely due to the algorithm and keyword search tool. My initial post was just an introduction, informing everyone that I'll be sharing details and updates on

Rutledge City's serial killer, whom I've dubbed the Shadow Stalker.

For now, I post:

Residents of Liam Harris' building report surveillance cameras are scattered throughout. Is Rutledge PD aware? Have they thoroughly canvassed, reviewed footage, and interviewed all tenants? This could be a breakthrough. #shadowstalker #rutledgemurders.

CHAPTER 8
CARTER

I adjust my glasses, squinting and battling the glare of the monitor, as I delve into the comments of the latest post from the Shadow Stalker Updates page. Detective Booker interrupts by knocking on my office door.

"Carter, get a load of this." Her voice is sharp, like a knife cutting through the monotonous hum of the station. My eyes flick up from his own screen as I watch Booker thread her fingers through her hair, worry etched into lines on her forehead. She motions for me to follow her back to her desk to review what's on her screen. The discussion amidst blaring telephones and rustling papers offers an interesting contrast to the usual chatter about case updates or irrelevant small talk.

I take over and navigate to the post she mentions, reading aloud for my partner's benefit. "Residents of Liam Harris' building report surveillance cameras are scattered throughout..." I trail off as I click on an attached image showing a grainy shot of what looks like said security cameras. The ones the department is currently working on getting a subpoena for.

"Whoever posted these must've got someone

inside," Booker states matter-of-factly, leaving no room for argument. It's clear now that we're not dealing with just another obsessed civilian but someone much more invested.

"A good Samaritan?" I joke, dry humor punctuating my words before asking further questions to get a fuller picture of whoever might be behind this bold move - even if it turns out to be reckless curiosity.

"No....more likely a Villain masquerading." Jenkins grumbles within earshot and casts meaningful glances towards us both. Jenkins is an older and more seasoned detective known for skepticism. There's shared laughter around and some nods echoing Jenkin's sentiment but I keep scrolling down looking for facts among local prejudices and idle chatter – something that could help build our fledgling profile of the anonymous detective.

The tension doesn't lessen any, but between these moments, there's intense anxiety in the room.

"Let's see how long they can hold their own," I murmur to myself before turning to make my way back to the break room, the promise of a hot cup of coffee summoning me. I'm greeted by the comforting aroma of freshly brewed coffee mingling with the faint scent of disinfectant. The lights overhead cast a harsh glow over the room, illuminating the rows of mismatched mugs and the gleaming stainless steel Keurig machine standing sentinel on the countertop.

As always, there's a pot of brewed coffee left out which a member of our team manages to refill throughout the afternoon each day. I reach for a K-cup from the neatly organized rack, fingers lingering over the array of options before settling on a robust blend. My gaze drifts idly around the break room, taking in the familiar sight of my colleagues scattered throughout the space.

Detective Jenkins stands at the far end of the room, engrossed in conversation with Booker. Their voices blend together in a soothing murmur, punctuated by the occasional burst of laughter. I glance at the clock on the wall, noting the late hour. The precinct is quieter now, the frantic energy of the day gradually ebbing away as evening approaches.

Finally, the Keurig beeps, signaling that my coffee is ready. Back in my office, my fingers dance across the keyboard, attempting to dig up any information on the mysterious individual behind the Shadow Stalker Updates page. After savoring the last sip of my coffee, I navigate through various databases and social media platforms in search of any leads.

Despite its recent creation, the page has garnered a solid following, drawing in people from both within and beyond Rutledge. The comments are a mix of curiosity, fear, and skepticism, with many expressing a lack of faith in our precinct's ability to solve the murders plaguing our town.

I furrow my brow as I scroll through the page, feeling a knot of concern tighten in my gut. If the suspects catch wind that civilians are onto them, it could jeopardize our entire investigation. And then there's the issue of the surveillance camera footage they're referencing. Despite our efforts to subpoena the files, I know they no longer exist.

The profile offers no solid leads - no connections, no friends, just a growing list of followers. It's a dead end, and I'm left grappling with the frustrating reality that I can't dig any deeper without creating an account. But I have no desire to join the ranks of social media users, so I'm left lurking on the outskirts, unable to interact or gather crucial information.

As I close the browser window, a sense of unease settles over me. The clock is ticking, and with each passing moment, the elusive figure behind Shadow Stalker Updates slips further from our grasp. But I refuse to let frustration cloud my judgment. There's still work to be done, leads to follow, and justice to be served - even if it means navigating the treacherous waters of the digital world from the sidelines.

I rub my temples, trying to ease the growing ache behind my eyes. How does this anonymous individual know about our investigative details? It's like they're one step ahead of us, taunting us with their insider knowledge.

Harper and I are the last ones left in the precinct. Folders and papers clutter my desk as I sift through case files. "I think I'm gonna head home, Harper," I call out to her as she sits at her desk outside my door. Stretching my arms above my head I add, "you should do the same. We've been at this for hours."

Harper nods, her eyes heavy with exhaustion. "Yeah, you're right. I'll see you tomorrow, Detective." I gather my coat and briefcase, but as I step out into the cool night air, a nagging thought tugs at the back of my mind. Liam's building. Maybe someone there has seen something - someone out of place, someone suspicious. I make my way to the intersection of Main Street and Elm Avenue, the bustling city noises fading into the background as I approach the run-down apartment building.

The block is eerily quiet. Inside, I notice a figure huddled in the dimly lit corridor. It's a homeless woman, wrapped in tattered blankets, her eyes wary as they meet mine. "Evening, ma'am," I say, my voice gentle but firm. "I'm Detective Carter. Have you seen anyone strange lurking around here lately?"

The woman shifts uncomfortably, her gaze darting nervously around the deserted corridor. "Not really," she mumbles, her voice barely audible above the distant hum of traffic.

"Are you certain?" I inquire gently, leaning in slightly to emphasize the importance of her answer. "How long have you been here?"

"Just a few hours," she replies hesitantly, her voice tinged with uncertainty. "I can leave now."

"You were here the last time I passed through. It seems like you frequent this spot. I'd rather not have to bring you in for trespassing. Can you help me out?"

"Well, someone came by asking me a lot of questions."

"Can you tell me what they looked like? It's important."

She hesitates, chewing on her cracked lips before finally speaking up. "It was a woman," she says, her voice trembling. "Said she was a private investigator or something. Asked me a bunch of questions about the building owner."

My heart sinks at her words, confusion swirling in my mind. A private investigator? What would someone like that be doing snooping around here? She describes the woman's features in detail.

I thank her for her help, slipping a few dollars into her outstretched hand before making my way back to my car. The drive home feels long with the silence of the car enveloping me. This woman, the one the lady encountered in Liam's building, is undoubtedly the mastermind behind the Shadow Stalker Updates page, conducting her own investigation.

As I turn into my parking spot and cut the engine, the silence is broken only by the distant chirping of crickets. I'll delve deeper into this as the stakes are high; not only must I protect the integrity of our investigation, but I also have a duty to safeguard the safety and well-being of the residents of Rutledge. I let out a heavy sigh and make my way into the house.

CHAPTER 9
AILA

My heart races as I sprint through the dimly lit streets, the sound of my ragged breaths echoing in the deserted neighborhood. The abandoned homes loom, their shattered windows and crumbling facades casting shadows across the cracked pavement. I can feel his presence behind me. My legs ache but the adrenaline surges through me, urging me to run faster.

The distant sound of fast-paced footsteps grows louder. I glance over my shoulder, but the darkness obscures his face, leaving only the menacing silhouette of a tall and imposing figure. It's as if I'm trapped in slow motion, my limbs moving sluggishly against the oppressive weight of terror. I stumble, my feet caught on an uneven lift in the pavement sending me crashing to the ground.

I feel a sharp sting of pain in the knee used to brace my fall. My hands are covered in scrapes and peeled-back skin. I shriek in pain, as he closes in on me. A strangled cry escapes my lips and I raise my head to face his shadowy form looming over me. His hand tightens around the cold metal of a gun, his finger twitching on the trigger as he levels it at my head.

I squeeze my eyes shut, bracing for the explosion of gunfire, but instead, I'm jolted awake by the deafening sound of my own screams. I sit bolt upright in bed, drenched in sweat feeling relieved that it's yet another dream. The room is bathed in the soft glow of the pre-dawn light, casting long shadows across the walls.

Jaison's side of the bed is empty, the sheets rumpled from where he had lain moments before. I take a deep, shuddering breath, trying to calm my racing heart as I glance at the clock on the bedside table. It's just after 5 a.m., and he's already in the shower, preparing for another early morning at work.

As I sit there, trembling from the remnants of my nightmare, Jaison emerges from the bathroom, a cloud of steam billowing out behind him. He's dripping wet, water pooling at his feet as he rushes over to my side, concern etched on his face. "Another nightmare?" he asks, his voice soft with worry.

I nod, wrapping my arms around myself in a feeble attempt to ward off the lingering chill. "But this time... it was different. I could almost sense it was a dream before I woke up." Jaison's brow furrows in concern, but he doesn't press the issue. Instead, he dresses quickly for work and gathers his things to head out the door.

Alone now, I make my way to the shower, hoping the warm water will wash away the last traces of fear clinging to my skin. I feel a sense of calm begin to settle over me, easing the tension from my muscles. I decide to clear my mind with a jog. I lace my sneakers and head out the door, the cool morning air refreshing against my skin as I make my way to the city center park.

The park is a sprawling oasis in the heart of Rutledge. Tall trees line the winding trails, their branches reaching skyward in a canopy of vibrant green leaves. I follow the path as it winds its way through the park, the soft crunch of gravel beneath my feet gives a soothing rhythm as I lose myself in the beauty of my surroundings. Birds chirp overhead, their songs blending with the gentle rustle of leaves in the breeze.

I can feel more tension melting away, replaced by serenity. For a moment, I forget about the nightmares and the fear that has been haunting me. I take in the sights around me. People of all ages and backgrounds dot the landscape, each immersed in their own activities. Some sit on wooden benches, soaking in the tranquility of the surroundings. Others lounge on blankets spread out on the grass, basking in the warmth of the sun.

I watch as fellow runners zip past me, their strides strong and purposeful. Each one seems lost in their own world, their faces set with determination. It's as if they're oblivious to the dangers lurking in our town, or perhaps they're just determined to maintain a sense of normalcy despite the chaos that surrounds us. I can't help but admire their resilience. They're the brave ones, the ones who refuse to let fear dictate their lives.

After my invigorating jog through the park, I'm still buzzing with energy, so I decide to make a spontaneous trip to the gym. I approach the entrance, only to realize that I've left my gym bag and membership card at home. I'm forced to sign in at the front desk for a temporary card. The receptionist, a familiar face who knows me by name, smiles warmly as I explain the situation. Without hesitation, she issues me a temporary daily card, waiving the usual fee.

I've run into the morning rush and I'm greeted by the a hum of activity and the sound of weights clanking. It's a hive of motion, with people of all fitness levels sweating it out on various machines and equipment. Despite the crowded space, I scan the room, hoping to catch sight of Hank, the elderly gentleman who often patronizes the gym for early morning workouts. However, today, he's nowhere to be found among the bustling crowd.

I decide to forge ahead with my workout. Skipping the treadmill, I head straight for the leg press machine. I push through a challenging leg workout, achieving my goals for the day. Feeling accomplished, I leave the gym and head home to freshen up.

After my shower, I slip into clean clothes and prepare a simple chicken Caesar salad for lunch. As I sit down to eat, my mind drifts back to my encounter with the homeless woman at Liam's building. Her mention of the building's owner being a slumlord piques my curiosity, so I pull out my phone to do some research.

A quick search reveals that the building is owned by NESKER REALTY GROUP. Intrigued, I delve deeper, searching for their office location in Rutledge. To my surprise, the address leads me to a small home, not an office building as I had expected. It seems NESKER REALTY GROUP operates out of a remodeled dwelling.

I decide to pay them a visit. When I arrive, a woman answers the front door. She introduces herself as the owner's assistant.

"Hello. I'm conducting some inquiries regarding the building on Main Street. Would it be possible to speak with the owner?"

Her expression tightens, and she hesitates before responding, "I'm sorry, but the owner is not available for interviews at the moment."

"I understand, but I'm a community-appointed investigator, and I have some questions about the property.

It won't take long." She eyes me skeptically, then shakes her head.

"I'm sorry, but I can't help you. You'll have to leave."

"But wait, have you seen the recent updates on the Shadow Stalker's page? They mention issues with the building's security cameras." She scoffs, dismissing the page with a wave of her hand.

"That page is run by an idiot. The police department is aware that the cameras have no footage."

"But according to the page operator, the cameras seemed to be functioning. Can you explain that?" Her demeanor turns cold, and she takes a step back.

"I have nothing more to say. Please leave now, or I'll have to call the police." Feeling frustrated, I realize that this visit has only deepened the mystery surrounding Liam's building and its owner.

Maybe I've misjudged the situation. I could have sworn those cameras were working, judging by the bright lights illuminating them. But now, with this new information about disabled cameras, I'm starting to doubt my initial assessment. How long have they been out of commission? And why would someone go to the trouble of installing cameras only to not maintain them?

A sense of unease washes over me as I consider the implications. Could it be that these cameras are nothing more than a facade, a feeble attempt to give the illusion of security?

I stay back and keep a close eye on the office, settling into a booth at a nearby diner with a view of the building across the road. Ordering a light meal, I try to appear casual, but my mind is racing with thoughts. My gaze flickers between the steaming cup of coffee in front of me and the dull unit across the street.

Time seems to stretch endlessly as I wait for any sign of movement from the office. The minutes tick by, but there's nothing—not a single light flickering on or off, no shadow passing by the windows. I try to distract myself by nibbling on my food, but my mind keeps returning to the unanswered questions swirling.

As the evening wears on and the sky outside darkens, I feel a sense of frustration mounting within me. Hours have passed, and still, I have nothing to show for my efforts. It's as if the building itself is taunting me, daring me to uncover its secrets. Finally, with a heavy sigh, I admit defeat. It's clear that nothing will happen tonight, and I can't afford to waste any more time on this fruitless attempt. I settle the bill and make my way home.

There's a sense of release knowing that I can finally retreat to the safety of my own home. I quicken my pace, determined to beat Jaison back. The last thing I need is for him to question where I've been all evening. He's already expressed his concerns about my investigation, urging me to put an end to it before things get out of hand.

But I can't shake the feeling that I'm onto something—that there's more to this case than meets the eye. And despite Jaison's warnings, I can't bring myself to abandon it just yet.

CHAPTER 10
CARTER

I'm seated at my desk, surrounded by the low hum of ringing phones and the steady clack of keyboards. The precinct is alive with activity, but my focus is singular as I sift through the computer database. Harper bursts into the room, her expression urgent. "Carter, we've got a new one. Body found on Buckley Road."

My stomach tightens at the news. Another victim, another family shattered. I nod, already mentally preparing for the task ahead. The air in the room feels heavy with anticipation as if we're all holding our breath. "Any details?" I ask. Harper flips open her notepad, the sound of pages rustling filling the air.

"A close friend had prior plans with the deceased. Stopped by when he didn't show and was not answering calls." I nod, exchanging a somber glance with Harper.

"Alright, let's move. We need to get there fast."

We gather our gear and head out, the squad cars tearing through the streets with sirens blaring. The pressure is tense as we approach the scene. The neighborhood we're entering is quiet with rows of modest and larger-sized houses lining the streets. Each home has well-manicured lawns and neatly trimmed hedges framing the yards. I take in the sight of nice cars parked in the driveways, evidence of the wealthy families that call this district home.

"Remember, no one enters until we secure the area," I remind the team as we disembark. We fan out, securing the perimeter and assessing the situation. Inside, the scene is grim. The body of Henry "Hank" Easton lies sprawled on the floor, his lifeless form conflicting with the neatness of the surrounding room. Hank's face is twisted in a silent scream, his hands clutching at his chest in a futile attempt to protect himself. Defensive wounds mar his hands, evidence of a struggle against his attacker.

I crouch down beside the body, taking in the details. The knife wounds are precise and deliberate, indicating a calculated attack. It's clear that Hank put up a fight. Despite his advanced years, Hank appears to be in remarkable shape. His physique speaks of a life well-lived. A wave of sadness washes over me. Hank, a man in his mid-70s, had lived a long and undoubtedly full life. It's hard to fathom that someone would target him in such a brutal and senseless attack.

But I take in the scene before me and my mind race with possibilities. It doesn't make sense and I can't shake the feeling that this is the work of the city's shadow stalker. I pause, realizing the weight of the words I've just used. "Shadow stalker" – a name coined by the townsfolk to describe what is now undeniably a serial killer on the loose.

My palms grow clammy, and my heart hammers against my chest. It feels like the air has been sucked out of the room, leaving me gasping for breath. Suddenly, I stumble, my legs feeling like jelly. Just before I hit the ground, Booker's steady arms catch me, preventing a full-on collapse. She looks at me with concern, her brow furrowed.

"Detective Carter, are you alright?" she asks.

I nod weakly, trying to push past the overwhelming sensation of nausea. "I'm... I'm fine," I manage to choke out, though my voice wavers. Booker helps me out of the house, grounding me as we step into the cool air. She shoots me a questioning look, silently urging me to share what's on my mind.

"It's just..." I begin, my voice trailing off as I struggle to find the right words. "This case, it's hitting me harder than I thought. I've been in this department for years, but... but this, this is different. It's like the weight of it all is starting to crush me."

Booker listens intently, her expression softening with understanding. "It's okay, Carter. We all have our breaking points. Maybe it's time to take a step back and catch your breath. You can't help anyone if you're not taking care of yourself first." I nod and take a deep breath, trying to push aside the overwhelming dread.

A sleek SUV skids to a halt, gravel crunching under its tires. A young woman leaps out and her frantic movements immediately catches the attention of officers nearby. She charges toward the house, ignoring the crime scene tape. Officers swiftly move to block her path.

"Please! That's my grandpa in there! I need to see him!" Her voice trembles while tears stream down her cheeks. My heart clenches as I watch her agony unfold. The raw pain of loss tearing at the fabric of her soul. But even as her cries pierce the air, duty demands that I remain composed.

"Ma'am, I'm sorry, but you can't go in there," one of the officers says gently. "We need to secure and assess the scene." Her sobs increase, echoing through the chatter amongst the onlooking crowd as spectators attempt to comfort her.

Stepping back into the house, the atmosphere is charged with the intensity of the investigation. My colleagues move purposefully around the room, meticulously cataloging each detail of the crime scene. Their voices blend into a low murmur, punctuated by occasional calls for evidence collection. I strain to catch fragments of conversation. "Possible struggle," one voice murmurs, while another calls out, "No sign of forced entry."

I make my way through the room, my gaze sweeping over every surface with practiced precision. In the midst of this careful scrutiny something catches my eye—a glint of light, subtle yet unmistakable. Bending down, I feign interest in a stray piece of debris, my fingers skillfully concealing the telltale earring hidden beneath. With ease, I slip it into my pocket for later examination.

Straightening up, I glance around the room, ensuring no one has witnessed my covert acquisition. My actions go unnoticed so I join Booker and the rest of the team. They're collectively focused on determining the suspect's entry point. Booker's voice cuts through the noise, "You would think people would start locking their doors overnight in this town after everything that has transpired." A few of us signal our agreement.

Back at the station, the air is tense as we gather to discuss our next moves. Booker's concerns weigh heavily as we contemplate the grim reality of four meticulously executed murders, all with a chilling precision that hints at a single perpetrator. The consensus among the team is clear: we're facing a serial killer.

The only pattern we can discern is that the victims appear to be single and vulnerable. After much deliberation, we agree that it's crucial to address the media. Keeping the public informed is important, even in the face of such chilling circumstances. It's decided that I'll be the one to deliver the live press briefing later this afternoon.

Seeking a moment of solitude, I retreat to my office. Harper, always attentive, offers her assistance. "Can I get you anything, Detective? Maybe even a sealed energy drink?" she quips, trying to lighten the heavy mood. I appreciate her offer but decline, needing some time alone to process my thoughts.

As I stand before the podium, the bright lights of the press briefing room bear down on me. Reporters sit poised with their pens ready, while concerned citizens fiddle in their seats.

"Ladies and gentlemen of Rutledge, I come before you today with a heavy heart to address a matter of grave concern to our community. Over the past weeks, we have been faced with a series of brutal and meticulously planned murders that have shaken us to our core." I scan the room, briefly making eye contact with multiple members of the audience.

"After careful consideration and investigation, it has become apparent that we are dealing with a serial killer. This individual has shown a chilling level of ruthlessness, targeting single and vulnerable individuals in our community. I understand that this news is alarming and unsettling, but I want to assure you that the Rutledge Police Department is fully committed to bringing this perpetrator to justice. We are sparing no effort in our pursuit of the truth, and we will not rest until we have apprehended the person responsible for these heinous crimes.

In the meantime, I urge all residents to remain vigilant and take precautions to ensure their safety. If you notice anything suspicious or have any information that could assist us in our investigation, please do not hesitate to come forward.

Together, as a community, we will overcome this challenge and emerge stronger than ever. Thank you for your attention, and may we all stay safe in these troubling times."

I brace myself for the incoming questions. "Detective Carter, can you shed any light on the motive behind these killings?" one reporter calls out, their voice echoing in the hushed room. I take a moment to gather my thoughts before responding.

"At this time, we are still working to understand the motive behind these senseless acts of violence. However, it appears that the perpetrator is specifically targeting single and vulnerable individuals within our community. It is no secret that all of the victims to date have been men."

Another voice rises from the crowd, this time belonging to a concerned citizen. "What steps are the police department taking to ensure our safety?"

"We have increased patrols in the affected areas and are collaborating with other law enforcement agencies to pool our resources and expertise."

A sudden interruption cuts through the air. A citizen stands up, their voice shaking with anger and frustration. "Why are you just telling us about this serial killer now? Are you even keeping an eye on the Shadow Stalker page? They're the only ones being honest with us!"

The room erupts in chaos, everyone chiming in with their own opinions and worries. Staff scrambles to regain control, begging for order.

"Please, calm down," one of them pleads. Meanwhile, I stand at the front, trying to stay composed despite the onslaught of criticism. I get it – they're scared, they want answers. But now isn't the time to argue.

I take a deep breath, trying to quiet the room with a raised hand. "I hear you," I say, my voice cutting through the noise. "We're doing all we can to keep you safe. We're on it, and we're checking out the Shadow Stalker page too." Gradually, the voices in the room begin to quiet, replaced by a tense silence as the crowd waits for my next words.

"In closing, I want to reassure everyone that we are taking this situation very seriously. I urge you all to remain alert and to report any unusual activity. Together, we can keep our community safe. Thank you for your cooperation and understanding during this challenging time. Our hearts go out to the victims' families." As the press briefing comes to an end, I step back from the podium, feeling a mixture of relief and overwhelm. I realize that this shift in the case is just the start of a lengthy journey ahead.

CHAPTER 11
AILA

The scent of freshly baked peach cobbler fills the air in my kitchen. I catch the muted tones of the television from the adjacent living room. The news anchor's voice rings, accompanied by footage of Carter delivering the press briefing I've been eagerly awaiting. As I watch, I feel a flicker of vindication—I had sensed the presence of a serial killer lurking in Rutledge long before the authorities acknowledged it. But that feeling is quickly overshadowed by sorrow and dread.

The latest victim, revealed to be Hank from the gym, saddens me. I had been exercising in the gym with him just days ago, never imagining that he would become the target of such senseless violence. I refuse to sit passively while the shadow stalker continues to prey on innocent lives.

The evening settles as I prepare to call it a night. Reaching out to the cleaners who stumbled upon Jacob Garcia's lifeless body is the first thing on my agenda for the morning. I spend a few moments on my night routine, washing my face, exfoliating, and finishing with a gel moisturizer. I brush my teeth and tie my hair back before covering it with a silk bonnet and climbing into bed.

A quick search in the morning yields the name of the company—a small, family-run operation catering to the upscale residents of Rutledge. I dial the number and brace myself for the conversation ahead. A woman's voice answers, her words hesitant as she announces her limited English proficiency. Undeterred, I ask if someone can translate, and soon, her cousin joins the call.

Through broken English and halting phrases, they recount the events surrounding Jacob's tragic demise. His affluent lifestyle, fueled by his success as a realtor and social media influencer, paints a picture of a man living on the edge. Parties, drugs, and a carefree attitude defined his existence, making his death seem almost inevitable.

As they speak, I listen intently, absorbing every detail like a sponge. Their words confirm my suspicions— Jacob's death was not a random act of violence, but rather a consequence of his risky behavior. He often met individuals online and brought them back to his home.

Pretending to be a private investigator, I carefully navigate the conversation, coaxing out information while maintaining the facade of professionalism.

"So, it's possible that Jacob brought a woman home that night? Who might have taken off early leaving him vulnerable and insecure in his home?' I ask.

"Mr. Garcia, he bring people to home. Men and women, many times. We clean, morning come, and still some people there, sleeping. They no wake up," he clarifies.

The thoughts swirl in my mind as I try to make sense of it all. I ponder whether the police department possesses this crucial information and has taken action upon it. They could investigate his online dating profiles to determine if he had arranged any meetings. The cleaners have been the most cooperative in divulging details to me, and I'm certain they've shared everything with the authorities. It's plausible that the department has already explored these leads, especially since Jacob's murder was the initial documented one. Perhaps all their efforts led to dead ends.

It's possible that Jacob might have picked someone up randomly at a nightclub or bar that night, and the encounter wasn't initiated through online profiles. The perpetrator clearly had malicious intent, evidenced by their decision to drug him before strangling him, presumably to minimize resistance. Maybe the strangulation was an attempt to conceal a night of drug-fueled activities gone awry.

So many questions linger unanswered. Yet, despite their differences, there's no apparent connection between Jacob, Liam, Daniel, and now Hank, besides their status as single men. It's highly unlikely that 74-year-old Hank sought companionship through dating apps. Daniel was known to be aloof, preferring solitude. Liam, as neighbors described, drowned his sorrows in alcohol daily. There's no evidence to suggest the presence of a dating app killer. Something inconspicuous links these men together. I conclude the call and thank them for their time.

I dedicate several hours to combing through online profiles in search of Liam's ex-wife. Her name has been making headlines lately, ever since she declined to provide any statements to the media. After some digging, I stumble upon a profile that's kept private, except for a couple of photos serving as the main avatar and header.

The header image catches my attention immediately. It features a brunette woman, likely in her mid-40, embracing two teen girls. Both girls sport blonde hair and striking grey eyes. But what really grabs my attention is the older girl's uncanny resemblance to Liam. From the shape of her forehead to the curve of her nose, she could easily pass for his daughter. It's evident that these girls are likely his, and the woman in the photo must be her.

I decide to follow her profile. Despite the privacy settings, I'm hopeful that my follow request will catch her eye. After all, given the recent media attention surrounding Liam's death, she's probably flooded with requests and messages. Nonetheless, I take the chance, crafting a carefully worded introduction in the hopes of initiating contact.

Shadow Stalker Updates: I hope you're hanging in there amidst everything. I'm a local investigator here in town. I've been following what's been going on with Liam's passing, and I can only imagine how tough it must be for you and the girls. I stumbled upon your profile and couldn't help but notice how much your daughters resemble Liam. I know he meant a lot to them, and I just wanted to reach out and offer my condolences. I'm not trying to pry, but I'm really just trying to piece together some things. Liam's death has got everyone on edge, and I'm trying to do what I can to prevent anything like this from happening again. I figured maybe you could shed some light on his life and help us understand a bit better. I totally get it if you're not up for chatting, but if you're open to it, I'd love to hear from you.

As I sift through the clutter of profiles, I stumble upon an outdated account that appears to belong to Liam Harris. The page offers a glimpse into a past life frozen in time. There he is, smiling in each photo, a picture of familial bliss alongside his ex-wife and their two young daughters. In these snapshots they're a picture-perfect family, playing at the park, building sandcastles on the beach, and sharing meals at cozy diners.

But beneath the surface of these cheerful images lies a question that gnaws at me: what went wrong? Was it the divorce that shattered their peaceful façade? My mind flits to darker possibilities, contemplating the financial aftermath of their separation. Could Liam's ex-wife stand to gain from any life insurance policies he may have held? It's a motive, perhaps, but not enough to cast suspicion without further evidence.

The abrupt rumble of an engine outside jolts me from my trance, signaling my husband's return home. I close my laptop and leap from the bed, arranging myself on the loveseat in the living room. I pretend to show interest in the sitcom playing on the television, masking the thoughts swirling beneath the surface.

CHAPTER 12
CARTER

The precinct hums with the usual activity, officers move purposefully about their duties. I barely register the commotion until the sound of frantic footsteps nearing draws my attention. A woman bursts through the doors, her tear-stained face a contrast to the otherwise stoic atmosphere of the precinct. Her hands are trembling in distress as she demands answers.

"Whoa, slow down," I say, moving to intercept her before she can cause further chaos. "Let's talk this through." She's frantic so her words tumble out with a rush of emotion. She accuses the department of withholding information about the serial killer, convinced that her grandfather could have been saved if we had acted sooner.

I recognize her as Hank Easton's granddaughter from the crime scene. "I understand you're upset. We're doing everything we can to catch this guy."

She shakes her head. "It's not enough. My grandfather deserved better." And she's right. No amount of reassurance can undo the pain of her loss. I can only offer my condolences and a promise to do everything in my power to bring his killer to justice.

"Come with me," I say, leading her to my office

where we can speak in private. Her eyes are red-rimmed and her hands still tremble as she takes a seat.

"Why didn't you tell us sooner?"

"It's not in the public's best interest for us to share every single detail with the community as to not jeopardize the case or potentially alert the suspect prematurely. The truth is, we're just as frustrated as you are."

"I just want to know why," she says, her voice barely above a whisper. "Why did he have to die like this?"

I don't have a simple explanation that could ease her pain. There are no easy answers in a case like this. "We'll find out what happened to your grandfather," I promise her. "And we won't stop until we do." I start delving into questions about her grandfather's personal life, but she stiffens defensively, expressing her discomfort with being interrogated by the very people she blames for her grandfather's death. I assure her that any insight she can provide might lead us closer to the truth and offer closure to her family. As she reluctantly shares memories of Hank, I listen intently, hoping each detail will help unravel the mystery surrounding his life and death.

"He was a kind-hearted man," she murmurs sadly. "He loved fitness, fishing... He had plans to go fishing with a friend that morning."

Her mention of a friend catches my attention, sparking curiosity about this individual's role in the events leading up to Hank's demise. "Can you tell me more about this friend?" I inquire. She hesitates, clearly struggling to recall details.

"I don't know much about him, to be honest. But he was the one who found my grandpa when he didn't show up for their fishing trip. He got worried and went to check on him."

"Thank you," I say earnestly. "Your cooperation means a lot." Gratitude flickers in her eyes, as she gathers her purse preparing to leave. I escort her from my office and down to the exit offering my condolences.

Moments later Booker storms into my office, with frustration etched in her expression. She updates me on the subpoena for the camera footage at Liam's apartment, confirming my suspicions that the request was unsuccessful. Our team received a response indicating there's no footage available. According to the owner, the footage automatically deletes to free up storage space, and it was batch deleted shortly after the incident occurred before he realized there was a need to preserve it.

"Very convenient," Booker spits out.

"It is," I agree, my frustration mirroring hers.

"I bet if we hauled them all in here it'd be different. I wouldn't be surprised if someone from his team suddenly had a change of heart under the right pressure."

"Are you seriously considering him a suspect? What does he stand to gain from all of this?"

"Who knows. I've stopped by the building and that office of a home. Plenty of neighbors have labeled him as greedy and shady. Perhaps he had a falling out with Liam and—"

I cut her off, my tone firm. "You visited his office?" I inquire, my eyebrows raised in surprise.

Booker shifts uncomfortably, realizing she may have said too much. "Well, yeah. I wanted to possibly talk to him," she admits reluctantly.

"And you didn't think to notify me?"

"I planned to, but it slipped my mind when I didn't find anything."

"The fact that the owner might have a motive for targeting Liam doesn't explain the other attacks," I reason, my voice stern. "No more off-the-record visits, Booker. Consider this your only warning."

Her shoulders slump in defeat. "Understood," she replies quietly.

"I'm assigning you to interview a friend of Hank Easton's. This friend was supposed to accompany him on a fishing trip the morning he was discovered. Let's delve deeper into this aspect of the case and see if there's more to it than meets the eye."

"On it," she says before turning to exit. As she walks away, I can't shake the nagging feeling in the pit of my stomach. Her unauthorized visit to the owner's office strikes me as more than just an innocent oversight. It's a breach of trust, a deviation from the protocol that dictates our every move in this investigation. If she's willing to go behind my back once, who's to say she hasn't done it before? What else has she done behind the scenes

As the lead detective on this case, I rely on my team to follow my lead, to trust in the process that we've built. But Booker's solo venture into the owner suggests a lack of faith in our methods, a disregard for the chain of command that threatens to undermine the integrity of our investigation. How many secrets has she hidden, waiting to be uncovered? I realize that I can no longer afford to turn a blind eye to Booker's actions. It's time to rein her in and ensure she's not undermining my own efforts.

I'm determined to address the Shadow Stalker Updates page. It disrupting our investigation with every post. The operator's sly tricks are only digging them deeper into trouble, and it's time to put a stop to it. With a reluctant sigh, I create a page for reporting, knowing it's our only recourse.

Pulling down the page won't be easy; they've been careful to skirt the edges of legality. They've made it clear they're independent from the department, operating on alleged information and opinions. It's a frustrating dance around the law, but one we have to navigate carefully.

Setting up the page under my personal information feels like a risk, especially considering the potential discovery from friends, family, and most importantly, my wife. I opt to go faceless knowing it's a risk I have to take. I spend a few tense minutes flagging numerous posts on the page, citing false information and the chaos it's incited. The system assures me my reports have been received and will be investigated, but whether they'll take action remains unknown.

CHAPTER 13
AILA

I find myself nestled in a cozy corner of the coffee shop just a few feet away from my building. The atmosphere here is serene, with the gentle hum of conversation and a comforting aroma of freshly brewed coffee and warm pastries. I've chosen a French blend today, with just a hint of sugar and cream to complement the rich flavors, accompanied by a crunchy blueberry muffin.

The shop itself is relatively quiet, save for the occasional clatter of dishes and the soft tapping of keys from a woman engrossed in her work on a laptop, likely taking advantage of the free Wi-Fi. The staff move about with practiced efficiency, their warm smiles adding to the inviting ambiance.

As I take a moment to savor my coffee, my phone buzzes with a notification, jolting me from my thoughts. It's a direct message on Echo, and my heart quickens with anticipation as I quickly unlock my phone and launch the message from Liam's ex wife.

I appreciate your efforts to reach out to me during this difficult time. I fully support the Shadow Stalkers page

and its mission to track down the person responsible for the recent tragedies in our city. It's crucial for the safety of everyone in our community, including myself and my girls. However, I must be honest about my feelings towards Liam and his untimely demise. While it's heartbreaking to lose someone, especially in such a tragic manner, I can't deny that Liam brought some of this upon himself. He made choices in his life that ultimately led to his downfall.

Liam had certain tendencies and behaviors that were unacceptable, to say the least. His inappropriate fetish put a strain on our marriage and ultimately led to our divorce. I had to prioritize the safety and well-being of myself and our children, which meant distancing myself from him. Additionally, Liam's drinking habits had become increasingly problematic over the years, and he had become complacent and lazy.

Despite my efforts to help him, he refused to change his ways. While I wish I could provide more assistance in your investigation, I haven't spoken to Liam in years, and I have no knowledge of his recent activities or acquaintances. I kindly request that most of what I've shared remain private, as I'm not willing to subject myself or my children to any unnecessary attention or scrutiny. Thank you for understanding, and please let me know if there's anything else I can do to assist you.

. I sit back in my chair, taking a moment to digest the new information. It's clear from her message that Liam's ex-wife isn't comfortable delving into the details of his past. I don't want to push her further and risk closing off any potential avenues of information. However, her mention of a fetish piques my curiosity. It's an unexpected revelation, and I wonder what she's alluding to.

I decide not to press the matter any further for now. Instead, I draft a simple response, expressing my gratitude for her insight and wishing her well. There's no point in dwelling on it at the moment; I'll have to dig deeper into Liam's history to unravel this.

Shifting my focus, I glance at my calendar and realize that I have a hair appointment scheduled with my stylist later today. It's a welcome change of pace from the intensity of the case, a chance to indulge in a bit of self-care and shake off the weight of my investigation. This case may be fraught with challenges, but it's also brought a newfound excitement to my otherwise mundane life.

The door jingles as I slip into the busy salon, leaving behind the chaos of the outside world. The air inside is heavy with the scent of various hair products giving off a sweet and floral aroma. This place is my sanctuary, where I can momentarily escape the stress of reality. Maria, my trusted stylist, beams at me as I enter, her eyes quickly catching the telltale signs of neglect in my hair.

"Looks like someone needs a touch-up," she observes, her voice soft with a smile. She gestures me to settle into the plush chair. We chat briefly about the look I'm aiming for, weighing different options before settling on a deep, jet-black dye to hide the rebellious brown roots starting to peek through. Maria warns me about the upkeep that such a bold change demands, stressing the importance of regular touch-ups to maintain the color's vibrancy. Despite her cautionary words, I'm steadfast in my choice. I yearn for the renewal that comes with shedding the remnants of my former self.

She starts her work and our conversation drifts

from the latest fashion crazes to the juiciest bits of local gossip. But inevitably, our talk circles to the Shadow Stalker case, a topic that has both terrorized and captivated our community. Maria's frustration with the stagnant investigation mirrors my own. She voices her doubts about the police's handling of the case, questioning how the Shadow Stalker page could possess such elaborate details about the victims. She suspects the perpetrator might be closer to the crimes than it seems.

Her skepticism strikes a chord with me, igniting unease that I can't quite shake. "It's unnerving, isn't it? I mean, how else would they have all that information?" Maria muses, her brow wrinkled in thought. "It's like they're doing the police's job for them." I offer a weak nod of agreement as my mind races and the hairs on my neck stand on end.

"I guess it's possible. Maybe they're just doing their own detective work. It's... commendable, in a way."

Maria agrees, her eyes reflecting a glimmer of respect. " Whoever's running that page, they're on the brink of cracking this case wide open. You'll see."

I manage a strained smile. As Maria puts the finishing touches on my hair, she swivels my chair to face the mirror, revealing her hard work. I'm taken aback by the transformation. The jet-black hue frames my face beautifully, though I can't help but notice how it seems to leech some warmth from my caramel-toned complexion. Still, I can't deny that I love it.

After rummaging through my purse for the cash I withdrew earlier, I thank Maria for her skillful work, feeling a weight lift from my shoulders as my time here is up and I won't be subjected to further discussions about the case.

Outside, the night air feels chilly, and the streets are

quiet under the soft glow of streetlights. I walk back home, my heels clacking against the pavement of the sidewalks. Thoughts from the day buzz around all confusing. Getting home feels like a relief. The cozy light from my lamps welcomes me. I sink into my comfy loveseat, but my mind keeps replaying everything. With a sigh, I grab my laptop, ready to dig deeper but I'm overcome by a rush of sleepiness that I lack the strength to fight off. Finally, exhaustion pulls me under, dragging me into a deep sleep.

CHAPTER 14
CARTER

I lean against the worn wooden desk in the precinct, surrounded by colleagues. The guys have drawn my mind back to a previous night, where I found myself out with the them for drinks. Detective Jenkins teases about my awful performance in our impromptu game of pool.

"Come on, Carter, you couldn't sink a ball if your life depended on it!" Jenkins laughs, slapping me on the back.

I chuckle, admitting, "I'm not exactly a pool shark. Didn't spend much time on that in college."

Curiosity piqued, the other detectives turn to me, eager to hear about my college days. With a grin, I confess, "Well, let's just say I was more of a ladies' man. Spent a lot of time charming."

Laughter ripples through the room as we share stories and jokes, bonding over shared experiences.

Suddenly, the cheerful atmosphere is interrupted by the arrival of Detective Booker. She strides into the room with a serious expression.

"Hey, can I talk to you alone for a minute, Carter?"

I comply, gesturing for her to follow me into my

office. Once inside, Booker wastes no time getting to the point.

"I've been doing some further research into the background of each murder victim," she begins, her voice tense. "And I've discovered something... unsettling. They're all registered sex offenders."

My eyebrows shoot up in surprise.

"I don't know how this was missed before, but I couldn't just ignore it. It feels like a significant piece of the puzzle."

"Why are you conducting your own investigation again?" I ask with concern.

Booker trembles slightly at the accusation. "It's not a side investigation, Carter. I spoke to Hank Easton's friend like you asked, and it led me in this direction. I couldn't just sit back and do nothing." I sigh, recognizing Booker's dedication to the case, though the information doesn't come as a shock to me.

In my relentless pursuit of answers, I delved deep into the murky pasts of the men who had fallen victim to the Shadow Stalker's twisted games. The more I uncovered, the more disturbing the truth became. Hank Easton, once a respected member of the community, harbored a dark secret from his youth. A prior conviction for harassment, stalking, and sexual assault against a co-worker stained his record, resulting in a five-year prison sentence. However, he emerged from his incarceration determined to turn his life around, seeking solace in the quiet anonymity of Rutledge. According to those who knew him best, he lived a reclusive life, devoting his time to volunteer work at a local homeless shelter.

Daniel Edwards, another of the Shadow Stalker's victims, bore the scars of his own troubled past. A history of violence and manipulation marred his relationships, culminating in a conviction for sexual assault against a former girlfriend. Reports painted a disturbing picture of a man prone to explosive outbursts, using coercion and aggression to assert control over his victim.

Liam Harris, an addition to the Shadow Stalker's tally, carried the weight of a heinous crime that had shattered countless lives. Accused and convicted of sexual assault against a minor, he had spent sixteen long years behind bars paying for his sins. Now released back into society, he faced the daunting task of rebuilding his shattered life while bearing the burden of his past transgressions.

And then there was Jacob Garcia, whose fall from grace had been swift and merciless. Accused of engaging in non-consensual drug-fueled encounters, he had faced public scrutiny and condemnation. Despite retaining the services of a high-powered attorney, he had been unable to escape the consequences of his actions, receiving a three-year prison sentence and mandatory registration as a sex offender. Yet, his time behind bars had been short-lived, his early release granted on the basis of good behavior.

When I sifted through the details of their pasts, a chilling pattern began to emerge. Each of these men had been tainted by darkness. Yet, in the eyes of the law, they had served their time, paid their dues to society. But now, as the Shadow Stalker continued to prowl the streets of Rutledge, it seemed that their past sins had come back to haunt them in the most horrifying of ways. I couldn't help but wonder—was justice truly blind, or had it merely been biding its time, waiting for the perfect moment to strike?

I kept the unsettling details to myself, wary of the potential consequences of releasing them to the public. While part of me yearned to share my findings, I couldn't shake the nagging fear that it would only serve to fuel the

Shadow Stalker's twisted ego. What if the town hailed them as a hero, a vigilante striking back against those they deemed deserving of punishment? The thought left me anxious, and I couldn't bear the idea of the Shadow Stalker growing bolder in the face of praise.

I'm jolted back to reality by Booker's abrupt declaration. "We need to notify the public," she insists, her voice edged with urgency. "Everyone on our registered offenders list needs to be aware and remain alert."

I struggle to find the words to respond, my mind racing with the potential repercussions of such a move. "No," I finally manage to utter. Booker's reaction is immediate, shock evident as her mouth drops open and her eyes widen in disbelief. "Are you kidding me?" she exclaims in frustration.

"It could be dangerous, Booker," I counter. "We can't risk inadvertently encouraging the killer. We're making progress just by knowing this information. We have a list of potential targets; let's start there. We can increase patrols in the areas where they're likely to strike."

"That's ridiculous. We don't have the manpower."

"Then we'll focus on the high-risk offenders. They are more likely to be attacked."

But..." Booker begins but her protests are cut short by my unwavering resolve.

"The decision is final," I state firmly with a tone leaving no room for argument. For a moment, there's a silence between us as Booker processes my words. Then, with a resigned sigh, she nods in acceptance. "Fine. But if anything happens..."

"We'll deal with it," I assure her, though the weight of my own uncertainty hangs heavy.

CHAPTER 15
AILA

I slip into the pool, letting the cool water envelop me as I swim laps to release the tension brewing in me. Each stroke feels like a small escape from the heavy weight of the past few weeks. The recreation center is quiet at this late hour, and the rhythmic sound of water against the tiles is strangely calming. I emerge at the pool's edge to catch my breath and rest for a moment. My heart lurches in my chest at the sight of a man towering over me. I blink rapidly, trying to clear my vision, but the dim lighting makes it difficult to see.

Before I can react, he grabs a handful of my hair and forces my head underwater. I panic as I struggle against his grip, but his strength is overwhelming. The water blurs into darkness. I fight against him, kicking and thrashing in a desperate attempt to break free. But it's no use. The water around me grows dark and thick as the dye from my hair fills it. My lungs burn as my vision starts to fade. I feel myself slipping away until I jolt awake with a gasp. I've soaked a fresh set of sheets in sweat. My husband stirs beside me, rubbing his eyes to strengthen his vision. He rubs my back slowly before wrapping me in his arms.

"Are you okay?" he asks. I rest my head against his chest in silence. "Honey, I think this is getting out of control. I suggest you get in touch with Dr. Gore," Jaison says.

Dr. Gore is a psychotherapist I started seeing after Jaison and I met. My mental health was a significant strain on our relationship back then. Both Jaison and Dr. Gore often described my behavior as self-destructive and impulsive. I struggled a lot with mood swings and anxiety, which made things difficult for both of us.

I suspect my current nightmares are triggered by the anxiety surrounding the case I'm working on. There's a deep fear brewing inside me, causing these intense dreams. It's been years since I last saw Dr. Gore, and the idea of going back to therapy makes me uneasy.

"Maybe you're right," I finally reply, my voice barely above a whisper. "I just thought I had it under control."

Jaison looks at me with understanding eyes. "There's no shame in asking for help, especially when things get tough."

I nod, feeling a mix of emotions. I know he's right, but the thought of revisiting those old wounds and talking about my fears again is daunting. The room feels heavy with the weight of our conversation, and I can sense Jasion's concern growing.

"Do you want me to call him for you?" he offers.

"No, I can do it," I say, trying to muster up some confidence. "I just need a little time to process everything."

He pulls me into a gentle hug. "Take all the time you need. I'm here for you, always."

"Thanks. I appreciate it." We sit in silence for a while, the only sound being our steady breathing.

After Jaison has left for work, I sit at the kitchen table with a cup of tea, staring at my phone. I scroll through my contacts until I find Dr. Gore's number and take a deep breath before dialing.

"Dr. Gore's office, how can I help you?" a friendly voice answers on the other end.

"Hi, this is Aila. I was a patient of Dr. Gore's a few years ago. I'd like to schedule an appointment," I say, my voice trembling slightly.

"Of course, Aila. Let me check his availability," the receptionist replies. After a brief pause, she continues, "We can fit you in next Tuesday at 3 PM. Does that work for you?"

"Yes, that works. Thank you."

"You're welcome. We'll see you then," she says before hanging up. I rush to log into the Shadow Stalker page. As the page loads, my heart sinks. A bright red banner flashes across the top: "This page has been disabled while under review."

I read the message twice, hoping I've misunderstood. But no, the message is clear. Echo has disabled my page due to multiple reports. It states that it is the platform's standard procedure to remove any page that receives such reports while they conduct a review. They've given me the option to submit supporting documents to help reinstate it. I stare at the screen, my blood beginning to boil. Who would report my page? My immediate suspicion falls on the suspect I've been trying to expose or, frustratingly, the police department itself.

"This can't be happening," I mutter to myself, feeling anger rising. The police should be supporting my efforts, not hindering them. After all, I've been doing their job for them, gathering information and sharing updates that keep the community informed and cautious. Fuming, I open a new document and start drafting a response to Echo. My fingers fly over the keyboard as I pour my frustration into words.

To whom it may concern,

I am the creator of the Shadow Stalker page on your platform. I am writing to express my deep disappointment and frustration over the recent disabling of my page. This page was created with the sole intention of assisting in the investigation of a dangerous individual who poses a significant threat to our community.

The Shadow Stalker page has not violated any terms of service or any laws. It has been a crucial tool in gathering and distributing information that has helped keep the community safe and aware. The reports against my page are unfounded.

I urge you to review the purpose and content of my page carefully. It does not promote violence or illegal activities. On the contrary, it aims to bring justice and ensure the safety of the community. Disabling this page undermines these efforts and only serves to benefit the very individual we are trying to stop.

Please consider this matter with the urgency it deserves. The community relies on the information provided by the Shadow Stalker page, and its absence could have dire consequences.

Thank you for your attention to this matter.

I sit back, reading over my words, before hitting send. The frustration still simmers, but I feel a small sense of relief having voiced my grievances. Why aren't the police on my side? It feels like I'm in this battle alone, and the very people who should be allies are working against me. If this doesn't get resolved soon, valuable time and information could be lost. Every minute counts.

I close my laptop. I need to clear my head. I grab my jacket and head outside. I'm met by the cool afternoon air and the rush of people and activity as the lunch rush roams about. As I walk, I consider my next steps. If Echo doesn't reinstate the page, I'll need to find another way to keep the community informed. Maybe a new platform, to maintain anonymity.

I take a walk to reset and I'm met with the cool afternoon air and the sight of people weaving through the sidewalks during the lunch rush. I quickly become lost in my thoughts, barely noticing those passing. Suddenly I'm jolted back to reality when a woman bumps into me, hard enough that my purse and keys go flying from my hands. "Oh, I'm so sorry!" she says, bending down to retrieve my things.

I crouch down too, reaching for my keys. "It's okay," I say, though I'm a little shaken up by the surprise. As I reach for my purse from her hands, our eyes meet, and I see a flicker of recognition in hers.

"May?" she says, her voice filled with surprise and hope.

I blink, taken aback. "No, I think you have me confused with someone else," I say, trying to keep my tone polite. My mind races, trying to remember if I've met her before, but nothing comes to the surface.

She doesn't seem convinced. "May, it's me, Barb.

We were part of the Between the Covers book club at the women's center on Brookhaven."

I furrow my brow, thoroughly confused now. "I'm really sorry, but my name is Aila, not May. I don't think we've met before."

Barb looks at me closely, her eyes scanning my face as if searching for something. "Are you sure? You look so much like her, just with a different hair color."

My frustration begins to bubble up. "No, I'm sure. I've never been part of a book club, and my name isn't May."

Her insistence is making me uncomfortable. She must sense it, because she backs off, her expression shifting from certainty to embarrassment. "Oh, I'm so sorry," she says, finally handing me my purse. "I guess I got it wrong. It's been a long time since I was at the book club."

She gives me an awkward smile, then turns and hurries off, leaving me standing confused and irritated. I watch her go, still trying to process the strange encounter. May? Book club? Brookhaven? None of it makes any sense. I'm not much of a reader, to be honest. The last book I finished was probably when I was a young adult. I don't go to libraries, and I definitely wouldn't join a book club.

Shaking my head, I tuck my keys and purse back into place and continue my walk. As I turn the corner towards home, I replay the conversation in my mind, trying to find any clue that might explain it. But all I find is more confusion. Who is May, and why does Barb think I'm her? Is it just a case of mistaken identity, or is there something more to it?

I push the thoughts aside. I have more pressing concerns right now, like getting the Shadow Stalker page reinstated and continuing my investigation. By the time I get home, I'm exhausted, both mentally and physically. I drop my keys on the kitchen counter and head straight for the shower, hoping the hot water will wash away some of the tension.

As I prepare dinner, I keep refreshing the page on my phone, hoping for a different message, but it remains disabled. The lack of updates bothers me, making it hard to focus on anything else. I stir the spaghetti sauce absentmindedly as the rich aroma of garlic and tomato sauce fills the kitchen. I plate the spaghetti and garlic bread and carry my plate to the loveseat in the living room, setting my phone on the coffee table within easy reach.

The news is on the TV, the usual blend of local updates and national headlines. I eat slowly, my eyes flicking between the screen and my phone. The anchor on the news mentions a recent development in the Shadow Stalker case, and my ears perk up. I lean forward, my heart racing. But it's just a recap of old information, nothing new, nothing helpful. I slump back against the cushions, pushing the spaghetti around my plate with my fork.

My phone buzzes with a notification, and I nearly drop my fork in my rush to grab it. But it's just a message from Jaison, not the update I was hoping for. I can't help the disappointment that washes over me. I reply quickly, setting the phone down again. The news anchor moves on to another story, and I let out a sigh, feeling defeated. The Shadow Stalker case has consumed so much of my thoughts and energy, and now with the page disabled, it feels like I'm hitting a brick wall.

I finish my dinner, the food tasting bland despite the effort I put into it. I set the plate aside and curl up on the loveseat deciding to call it a night.

INSOMNIA

CHAPTER 16
CARTER

I push open the front door, the familiar creak sounding louder than usual after the long, silent drive home. The house is quiet, except for the faint scratch of a pencil coming from the home office. I drop my coat on the hook by the door, feeling the day's fatigue settle deeper into my bones. The precinct had been a madhouse, as always.

"Hello," Phoebe calls from the office, her voice carrying a warmth that instantly starts to thaw the icy tension in my chest.

"Hey," I reply, making my way towards her. "It's late. Why are you still up?"

"I got a burst of inspiration," she says, looking up from her sketchpad with a radiant smile. "Decided to draw."

I step into the office, taking in the sight of her hunched over the desk, completely absorbed in her work. She turns her drawing towards me, revealing a haunting image of a tall, dark figure. It's not familiar and fills me with apprehension because of how eerily Phoebe managed to capture the danger and mystery.

"It's my interpretation of the Shadow Stalker," she

explains, watching my reaction closely. I raise an eyebrow, trying to keep my tone neutral.

"Interesting take."

She smiles, a little self-conscious, and starts tidying her pencils. "It probably doesn't match the descriptions you have, but it's how I imagine him."

We move into the living room, the plush couch a welcome comfort after the hard chairs at the precinct. I sink into it with a loud sigh. Phoebe follows, sitting beside me.

"The department is practically at a standstill with this one," I admit. "We're chasing shadows."

"I noticed the Shadow Stalker page is disabled. Maybe the person running it got scared or threatened."

I lean back into the couch, staring at the ceiling. "It's just another complication."

Phoebe kneels in front of me, helping me remove my shoes. Her hands are gentle, and I close my eyes for a moment, savoring the simple intimacy of the gesture. She starts to rub my feet, the tension slowly easing out of me. She removes my socks, pausing as she looks at my left foot.

"You know," she begins gently, "you've still never talked about your missing pinky toe."

I stiffen slightly, the memory of the incident flickering through my mind. I told Phoebe it was a work accident, and held off on details. It was too painful, too personal. "I'd prefer not to revisit such a traumatic memory," I say quietly. "If ever I feel comfortable sharing, I will."

Phoebe nods, understanding and compassion in her eyes. "I get it." She continues to rub my feet and we sit in comfortable silence for a while. My mind drifts back to the events of the day. The Shadow Stalker case is consuming all our resources. Every lead seems to dissolve into thin air, and the pressure is mounting. The captain is breathing down my neck, the media is relentless, and the public is scared. It's a nightmare.

Phoebe's voice pulls me back to the present. "You look like you're carrying the weight of the world on your shoulders."

"Sometimes it feels that way," I admit. "This case... it's like trying to catch smoke with your bare hands. Every time we think we have something, it slips away."

"I can't imagine how hard it must be. But you're the best detective I know. If anyone can solve this, it's you."

Her words are comforting, but the heaviness of responsibility is still overbearing. "Thanks, Phoebe. I just hope you're right." She gives me a reassuring smile and stands up, stretching.

"Come on, let's get to bed. You need rest."

I follow her to the bedroom and we both prepare for bed. The eerie drawing Phoebe made lingers in my thoughts. I know it's not an accurate depiction, but it captures the fear and uncertainty that this case has brought into our lives. We slide under the covers, and she curls up next to me.

As she drifts off, I lay awake, staring at the ceiling. My mind races. The case has taken a toll on everyone. The officers are exhausted, the victims' families are desperate for answers, and the town is on edge. It's a pressure cooker, and I'm the one expected to keep the lid on. Phoebe stirs beside me, her breathing deep and even. I envy her ability to find peace right now, amid chaos. I close my eyes, willing myself to sleep.

The next morning, the alarm pulls me from a restless sleep. I groan and rub my eyes, feeling the tiredness settle. Phoebe is already up, the smell of coffee drifting from the kitchen. I get dressed, my mind already shifting into work mode. Phoebe hands me a mug of coffee when I reach the kitchen. Today, I decide to spend an extra moment enjoying my breakfast from home and in the presence of my wife, who I feel distant from lately.

We talk about mundane things, trying to keep the conversation light. It's a small comfort, a way to maintain some normality. "I'll probably be home late again," I say as I grab my keys. "Don't wait up."

She offers a smile tinged with concern. "Be careful, okay?"

"I will," I promise, giving her a quick kiss before heading out the door.

The drive to the precinct is filled with the usual morning traffic. I listen to the R&B station on the radio, half paying attention. By the time I arrive, the precinct is buzzing with activity. I head straight to my desk, where a stack of files is waiting for me. My phone rings and I glance at the caller ID—it's one of the patrol officers. Something in the pit of my stomach tightens.

"Carter here," I say, pressing the phone to my ear.

"Detective Carter, we've got a situation at Rutledge City Center Park. You might want to get down here. Looks like the Shadow Stalker has struck again."

"I'm on my way." I grab my jacket and head out with racing thoughts. Another victim. Another piece of the puzzle, but at what cost? The drive to Rutledge City Center Park is tense. By the time I arrive, the scene is already cordoned off with yellow tape, and officers are scattered around, collecting evidence and taking notes. Jenkins meets me at the edge of the scene. "Detective, over here."

I follow him to a secluded area near the jogging path. There, lying in a pool of blood is an unidentified man. He appears to be in his thirties, dressed in running gear. There's a nasty gash on the back of his head, and beside him, a bloodied brick lies discarded on the ground.

"Looks like he was hit from behind while jogging," Jenkins explains, pointing to the brick. "No ID on him. We're still searching for evidence."

I nod, kneeling beside the body to get a closer look. The wound is severe, and it's clear he didn't see it coming. I glance around the park, taking in the serene surroundings now tainted by violence. The Shadow Stalker knows how to pick his spots—quiet, isolated places where no one would think twice about a jogger going missing.

"Get the brick bagged and sent to forensics," I say, standing up. "We need to find out who this guy is." The team works efficiently, but the lack of identification on the victim makes things harder. Hours pass as we scour the scene for any additional evidence, but there's nothing. No witnesses, no other clues. Just the body and the brick.

Back at the precinct, we run the victim's description through our system, but nothing comes up. It's like trying to find a needle in a haystack. The brick has been sent off for processing and could possibly return a positive DNA match.

Later that afternoon, we get a call from a new sports lounge, The Anchor. Their bartender skipped his shift, and his description matches our John Doe published on the local news channel and our Rutledge City Echo Page. A flicker of hope ignites in me as we arrange for the bar's manager to come in and identify the body.

An hour later, the manager, a middle-aged woman with a stern expression, arrives. I lead her to the morgue, and she takes a deep breath before stepping inside. The cold, sterile air hits us as we approach the body.

"That's him," she says, her voice trembling slightly. "That's Gary Robinson."

I comfort her, taking in the information. "Thank

you. Can you tell us more about him?"

"Gary was new to Rutledge," she begins. "He moved here from Brentley, Illinois. He was a good worker, kept to himself mostly."

"Do you know if he had any enemies? Anyone who might want to hurt him?"

She shakes her head. "No. I mean like I said he was fairly new. Says he relocated for a fresh start and never mentioned friends or family in the area. Think he might've been at the wrong place at the wrong time."

I thank her for her time and escort her out of the precinct offering my condolences. When I am back in my office, I take to my computer to search our criminal database and sure enough I find Mr. Robinson. My heart sinks realizing he fits the Shadow Stalker's MO perfectly. High-risk offenders, those the community might judge harshly.

Gary Robinson, a 34-year-old bartender with a dark past. Another victim discovered as the pieces are slowly coming together, but the picture they form is grim. I sit at my desk, staring at the board filled with photos, notes, and connections. Each victim, each crime scene, is a step closer to the department understanding the mind behind the madness. Phoebe's words from last night echo in my mind. "You're the best detective I know. If anyone can solve this, it's you." And I have. Now it's my duty to stay one step ahead of the team to bring the slaying to an end, singlehandedly.

I take a deep breath, steeling myself for the long road ahead. The next few days blur together in a frenzy of activity. We interview Gary's coworkers, neighbors, anyone who might have seen or heard something unusual. The forensic team works tirelessly to analyze the bloodied brick, searching for any trace evidence that might lead us to the killer.

Meanwhile, the town is on edge. News of the latest murder spreads quickly, and fear ripples through the community. People are scared to go out at night, worried they might be the next target, not fully understanding the MO of the killer. The media is relentless, hounding us for updates, speculating wildly about the identity of the Shadow Stalker.

In the midst of it all, I try to stay focused. One afternoon, as I'm concentrating on the case files in my office, Phoebe calls. "How's it going?" she asks gently.

"Slow," I admit. "We've identified the victim, but we're still trying to piece everything together."

"You'll get there," she says with unwavering confidence.

"Thanks. I needed to hear that."

"Come home soon, okay? You need to rest."

"I will. Promise."

After hanging up, I take a moment to clear my mind. I close my eyes, breathing deeply, trying to center myself. The case is consuming, but I can't let it break me. I have to stay strong, for Phoebe.

Forensics doesn't find anything outside of the victim's DNA on the brick. We canvass the area around Rutledge City Center Park again, this time with more focus. We question everyone and recheck every inch of the crime scene, looking for anything we might have missed. One of the officers finds a security camera on a nearby building. I offer to contact the owner at a later time to schedule a meeting to review the footage in depth. Booker questions the need to wait and suggests we go right over as a team and ask to review the footage right away. I have no sufficient rebuttal but I shoot her a glaring eye, displaying my disagreement with her undermining my efforts.

It's a long shot, but we pull the footage, the team hoping for a glimpse of the suspect. Hours of reviewing grainy footage doesn't pay off. The camera is situated near one entrance of the park on a storefront. We see people enter and exit the park throughout the day of the incident. However, because there are multiple exits from the center park, there is no way to pinpoint a suspect. The camera was not positioned to even catch a glimpse of the victim entering the park which proves he used an alternate entrance. I put on a facade of distress, but deep down, I'm finding some comfort in knowing that my efforts are not being shattered by my team.

CHAPTER 17
AILA

As I sit on the loveseat, I stare at the headline on my laptop screen: **Fifth Victim Found in Local Park – Gary Robinson Identified**. My heart pounds as I read through the article, detailing how Gary Robinson, a bartender at the new sports lounge, was found dead in the park where I often jog. The news says he was followed and attacked with a brick. I can't shake the memory of our brief interaction at the lounge. I remember feeling his eyes on me, a sense of unease creeping up my spine. Now, he's dead, and it feels like another personal connection to the Shadow Stalker case.

I take a deep breath, trying to steady my nerves. The anxiety nips at me and I know I have to do something. I can't sit idly by while another person falls victim to this killer. My thoughts race as I contemplate my next move. I need to step up my investigation.

I glance at my phone and see a notification from Echo. I quickly unlock my phone and launch the app with my fingers trembling slightly. The message reads: **Your Shadow Stalker Updates page has been reinstated. We apologize for the inconvenience**. Relief floods through me realizing my page is back online. I follow the link provided to log back into the page. The familiar layout greets me. I type out a new post, detailing the latest victim's information and urging the community to stay vigilant. I include a photo of Gary Robinson that I found online, hoping it will jog someone's memory or prompt them to share any information they might have of him. Apparently, Gary was new to Rutledge.

After hitting "post," I decide to head to the park where Gary was found. I need to see the scene for myself, to get a sense of what happened. I grab my jacket and keys and make my way to the door. I can't shake the feeling that I'm being watched. I pause and glance around, but the apartment is empty. Shaking off the paranoia, I step outside and head towards the park. The park is eerily quiet when I arrive. The usual sounds of children playing and dogs barking are absent. Instead, near the running path there's the remnants of a crime scene investigation. I walk along the path, my eyes scanning the area for any clues. I know the police have already combed through the scene, but I hope to find something they might have missed.

I reach the spot where Gary's body was found. The ground is still stained with blood. I kneel and examine the area, looking for anything out of place. There's not much between the pavement and the bordering grass and bushes. As I stand, I hear a rustling in the bushes. My heartbeats quicken and I instinctively reach for my phone. I slowly back away, keeping my eyes on the bushes. Suddenly, a figure emerges. I let out a sigh of relief as I recognize a small bunny, who's found discarded trash to nibble on. I decide it's time to leave. The park feels too unnerving, too filled with memories of what happened here.

When I get home, I immediately sit down with my laptop and immediately start researching Gary Robinson. I find his social media profiles, reading through his posts and looking for any connections to the other victims. Nothing stands out at first, but I keep digging, determined to find something. Hours pass, and my eyes grow tired from staring at the screen. Just as I'm about to give up for the night, my phone buzzes with a notification. It's a direct message on Echo from someone named Arias. I quickly open it.

Hey, I saw your post about Gary Robinson. I think I might have some information that could help.

I respond immediately letting Arias know that I am all ears and the information provided might help with the case.

I worked with Gary at the sports lounge. He was always a bit... off. There were rumors that he had a dark past, but no one knew for sure. Then one night, I overheard him talking to someone about the Shadow Stalker. He sounded almost... excited.

Did you see who he was talking to?

Not clearly, I only heard bits and pieces of the conversation. I just remember him finding it humorous and calling the department incompetent.

Did he ever talk about his past?

Not much. He's not from around here you know.

Rutledge is a nice but isolated city. I couldn't understand what brought him across the border into Ohio. Anyway, like I said he was strange and a few of us questioned his inappropriate behavior with some of the patrons.

What do you mean?

He flirted a bunch, but even when it became extremely uncomfortable to patrons and observers, he persisted. Borderline harassment.

Arias, thank you so much for this information. It's been truly helpful and I appreciate your willingness to assist in this matter.

Yeah, no problem. I've told that detective on the case. He barely asked any questions. He seemed more concerned with if anyone else had been lurking about the sports lounge or frequenting it. Didn't care much about what type of person Gary was. Either way, it's a tragedy and I am saddened by the loss.

Thank you again for your time. If you think of anything else, please let me know.

As I sift through the information, a pattern begins to emerge. Three of the five victims – Gary Robinson, the bartender; Daniel Edwards, from Trotter Rd and Liam Harris, who fell to his death– have been described by their acquaintances as strange and having exhibited inappropriate behavior. They weren't well-liked in their communities. Hank Easton and Jacob Garcia, on the other hand, were more well-regarded. The discrepancy is puzzling.

I lean back in my chair, tapping a pen against my chin. Maybe there's someone out there targeting these men for their actions. Perhaps it's a vigilante seeking revenge for something these men have done to them. Or maybe there's a connection between the victims that hasn't been uncovered yet. Determined to dig deeper, I decide to visit the sports lounge where Gary Robinson worked. If there's anything off about the place, it might give me a clue.

The sports lounge is bustling with activity when I arrive. The neon sign flickers, casting a blue glow over the entrance. I push open the door and step inside. The familiar scent of fried food and beer hits my senses. The noise is almost overwhelming – laughter, conversations, the clinking of glasses. It's hard to believe that just days ago, one of their own was found dead. I make my way to the bar, scanning the faces around me. Everything seems to be carrying on as normal, as if nothing has happened.

I spot a couple of bartenders chatting with customers, but there's no sign of Gary's absence affecting the atmosphere. I wonder if anyone here knows more than they're letting on. As I take a seat at the bar, I notice a familiar face across the room. My heart skips a beat. He's sitting with a companion at a table, nursing a drink, and looking around the room. My pulse quickens, and a sense of dread rises in my gut. I need to get out of here before he notices me.

I quickly stand up and make my way towards the exit, keeping my head down and avoiding eye contact. As I walk home, my mind wanders and I'm a bit shaken up. I realize that my trip today was fruitless as I hadn't had the chance to speak with any more of Gary's colleagues. I make a mental note to follow up at the lounge another time.

INSOMNIA

CHAPTER 18
CARTER

I sift through recent reports sitting at my desk in my office. The coffee in my mug has gone cold, but I barely notice. My phone rings with an incoming call.

"Carter," I answer, my voice gruff from lack of sleep.

"Detective Carter, the captain wants to see you in his office. Now." The voice on the other end says curtly. I hang up and stand, straightening my tie and taking a deep breath. Captain Walsh rarely calls for impromptu meetings, and when he does, it's never good news. I make my way through the busy precinct, nodding to a few colleagues as I pass.

The air is thick with the usual chaos – phones ringing, officers discussing cases, the hum of activity that never truly ceases. When I reach the captain's door, I knock lightly before stepping inside. Captain Walsh is behind his desk, his expression unreadable. He gestures for me to sit, and I comply, feeling a knot form in my stomach.

"Carter," he begins, his voice steady, "we need to talk about the Shadow Stalker case." I nod, waiting for him to continue. The captain leans forward, clasping his hands together on the desk. "Due to the lack of significant progress and the increasing number of victims, I've decided to make some changes."

My heart sinks. I know where this is heading. "Captain, if you just give me a little more time, I'm close to a breakthrough. I can feel it."

He shakes his head, his gaze unwavering. "We don't have the luxury of time, Carter. The public is scared, the media is breathing down our necks, and we need results. Effective immediately, I'm pulling you from the case and assigning Detective Booker as the lead investigator."

I feel like I've been punched in the gut. "Booker? Captain, she doesn't have the experience with cases like this. I've been on this from the beginning. I know the details, the patterns…"

Walsh raises a hand to stop me. "My decision is final. Booker has shown she's capable, and I believe she's in a better position to bring this case to closure." I open my mouth to protest again, but the look in his eyes tells me it's useless.

"Understood," I say, my voice tight with frustration. I stand and leave his office, barely managing to keep my composure. As I step out into the hallway, I see Detective Booker huddled in a corner with a few colleagues. She's smiling, clearly pleased with herself. It's obvious she already knows about the reassignment. Our eyes meet, and I can't help but glare at her. She looks back at me with a smug expression, and I know she had a hand in this decision.

I retreat to the isolation of my office, slamming the door behind me. The walls feel like they're closing in, and I pace back and forth, my anger boiling over. I throw my cold coffee into the trash with a force that sends the mug clattering. This was my case. I was supposed to stop the Shadow Stalker. Now, with Booker in charge, everything could fall apart.

I slump into my chair, running my hands through my hair. The fear gnaws at me – if Booker cracks the case, my reputation, my position, and everything I've worked for could be at risk. I've been meticulously piecing together things, following leads, and now it feels like it's all slipping through my fingers. Hours later, I finally head home, feeling defeated. Phoebe is waiting for me, her concern evident as soon as I walk through the door. "What happened?" she asks, her brow furrowed.

"I've been pulled from the case. They've assigned Booker to lead it now." Phoebe's eyes widen with shock.

Booker? But you're the one who's been working on this from the start! Why would they do that?"

"Captain thinks she's in a better position to bring the case to closure," I say bitterly. "She's been gunning for my spot for a while, and now she's got it." Phoebe shakes her head, her anger matching my own.

"I never trusted her. She's always been too eager to climb the ranks, no matter who she steps on." I sink into the couch.

"If she cracks this case, my spot might very well be up for grabs. Everything I've worked for could be gone."

Phoebe sits beside me, taking my hand in hers. "You're a great detective. You've solved so many difficult cases. This one is just... different. But you can't give up. Maybe there's still something you can do." Her words bring a small measure of comfort, but the weight of the situation still presses down on me.

"I just don't know what to do. I was so close..."

Phoebe squeezes my hand. "We'll figure it out.

Together. You've always been the one to uncover the truth, and I believe you still can." I nod but deep down, I know that time is running out. Booker will be diving into the case with fresh eyes, and if she makes a breakthrough, it'll be her name in the headlines, not mine. I need to find a way to stay involved, to keep my edge. It'll be a challenge to stay ten steps ahead. I'll lose access to most files and when my replacement is announced members of the town will be hesitant to speak with me. If I can figure out the Shadow Stalker's next move. I can stop them in their tracks.

The next morning, I wake up with a plan forming in my mind. I may be off the case officially, but that doesn't mean I can't continue my investigation unofficially. I get dressed and head to the precinct. When I arrive, I avoid Booker and the others, heading straight to my office. I close the door behind me and sit down, pulling out my notes.

Hours pass as I go over every detail, every report, every piece of evidence. Suddenly it hits me – I should pursue the victims of the murdered men. My access to the files related to this case has been revoked. So I'm forced to utilize my personal laptop and launch an internet search. It's not as efficient as the department's database, but it'll have to do. I start with Gary Robinson and work my way through the list.

It doesn't take long to find news articles and blog posts about most of the victims. The case of Liam Harris is more elusive. Because it involved a minor, details are scarce. I hit a wall, unable to find anything substantial online. I shift my focus to Jacob Garcia. It takes a bit of searching, but I eventually find an old article about his trial. He was accused of assault by multiple victims but only served thirteen months of a three-year sentence, thanks to a prestigious lawyer. His release caused quite an uproar in the community, and one name keeps popping up in connection with him: Channing Reid.

Channing Reid is very vocal about his encounter with Jacob Garcia. I find his social media profiles easily, and it's clear he hasn't let the past stay buried. He's made numerous posts about Garcia's recent death, calling it karma. One post stands out.

Justice may be slow, but it's relentless.

It's accompanied by a news article about Garcia's murder, and the comments section is filled with supportive messages from people who know Channing's story. Scrolling further, I see that Channing has started a support group for victims of sexual assault. He promotes it heavily online and hosts meetings at a local community center. One post announces a meeting scheduled for tonight. This could be my chance to get more information, maybe even speak to Channing in person.

I decide to go. I need to be discreet, though. I can't afford to draw attention to myself, especially now that I'm off the case. I grab my jacket and leave the precinct for the evening. The community center is an ordinary building on the outskirts of town. It's getting dark when I arrive, and I park my car a little way down the street to avoid suspicion. I walk up to the building, my heart pounding with anticipation. The door is slightly ajar, and I slip inside quietly.

I find the meeting room easily. There's a small window in the metal door, and I peek through it, careful not to be seen. The room is sparsely decorated, with a circle of chairs in the center. About a dozen people are seated, listening intently to someone speaking. There's a dark-haired woman, her back to me, but her presence commands the room.

I watch for a moment, trying to gauge the atmosphere. Her voice is calm but powerful, and the others seem to be hanging on her every word. When I catch a glimpse of her face, her presence catches me off guard. My gut tells me I must go, fast. In shock, I back away from the door and head outside. The cold night brushes the hair that has lifted on the back of my neck. I race home, panicking, trying to clear my mind of what I've witnessed. I'll come back later, maybe catch Channing after a meeting for a one-on-one conversation. For now, I need to regroup and plan my next steps.

CHAPTER 19
AILA

I arrive at Buckley Road, a peaceful and upscale neighborhood where Hank Easton used to live. The houses here are large and elegant, surrounded by meticulously maintained plots and tall trees. It's hard to believe that such a gruesome crime could occur in a place like this. I feel a pang of sorrow thinking about Hank; we used to work out at the same gym, often at the same time. He was always friendly so the news of his death hit me hard.

As I walk down the quiet street, I can't shake the feeling that someone here must have seen something. The houses are too nice, too equipped, to not have security cameras. I decide to start by knocking on the door of Hank's next-door neighbor. The house is impressive, with a large front yard and a tasteful porch. I take a deep breath and knock, my mind racing through the cover story I've concocted. After a moment, the door opens, and a middle-aged man with graying hair and a kind face peers out.

"Hello, can I help you?" he asks, his tone polite but curious.

"Hi," I say, forcing a professional smile. "I'm a private investigator hired by Hank Easton's family. They feel the police department is grossly mishandling the case, and they've asked me to look into it. Do you have a moment to speak?" The man's eyes widen slightly, and he steps back, inviting me inside.

"Oh, Hank was a good man. Please, come in." I follow him into a spacious living room, tastefully decorated with family photos and comfortable furniture. We sit down, and I lean forward, trying to project earnestness.

"Thank you for speaking with me," I begin. "I understand this must be a difficult time for everyone who knew Hank. His family is just desperate for answers." The neighbor nods, a sad smile on his face.

"Hank was sweet to us. He always had time to chat and always had a kind word. It's hard to believe he's gone."

"I'm so sorry for your loss," I say sincerely. "I was hoping you might have some information that could help. Do you have any security cameras that might have captured something?"

The man nods slowly. "Yes, we have a doorbell camera, but it doesn't capture too much of Hank's home. Our yards are quite large, so the camera's range is limited. It did, however, capture a figure entering Hank's yard the night he was killed."

I feel a surge of excitement. "Really? What can you tell me about this figure?"

He sighs, leaning back in his seat. "The build of the individual leads me to believe it's a woman, but I can't be sure. The detective who reviewed the footage said it was okay to delete it afterward." This strikes me as odd. Why would the detective allow such crucial evidence to be erased? And if the figure was likely a woman, why hasn't that information been made public?

"Can you describe the figure in more detail?" I ask, pulling out a notebook.

"The person was dressed in black clothing. They weren't very tall compared to the nearby parked cars and mailbox. I'd say they were likely between 5'3" and 5'6"."

"What makes you think it was a woman?" I ask, curious. He looks a bit embarrassed.

"Well, the figure was curvy. It was just an assumption based on that."

I nod, understanding. "Did the footage show how she entered or left?"

"She entered through the front. Hank must've let her right in; she never turned back to leave through the front yard. The footage doesn't show her departure, which means she must have exited through the back into the woods."

This is crucial information. I thank the neighbor for his time and stand up to leave. "You've been very helpful. I really appreciate it." As I walk back to my car, my mind is racing with possibilities. Who was this woman that Hank let in so willingly? I need to get this information out there, but I have to be careful. I don't want to jeopardize the investigation or put the neighbors in danger.

I sit in my car and pull out my phone, drafting a post for the Shadow Stalker page. I include the new findings, being careful to mention that it's alleged, preliminary, and not affiliated with the Rutledge PD.

New information has come to light regarding the recent murder of Hank Easton. A security camera captured a figure entering Hank's yard the night he was killed. The individual was dressed in black clothing and is believed to be a woman, based on her build. She was between 5'3" and 5'6" and entered through the front, indicating

that Hank might have known her. This information is preliminary and has not been confirmed by the Rutledge PD. Stay vigilant and report any suspicious activity.   #ShadowStalker   #HankEaston #RutledgeMurders"

I hit "post" and watch as the notification pops up, sending the update out into the world. Now, all I can do is wait and see if anyone comes forward with more information. I start the car and drive away, my mind buzzing with the new leads.

The next day, I decide to visit the gym where Hank and I used to work out. Maybe someone there remembers seeing him with a mysterious woman. I arrive at the gym and am greeted by the familiar sounds of weights clanging and people chatting. My attention is drawn in the direction of a few regulars at the gym. Hank often worked out in the earlier hours and beat the afternoon rush. It's a long shot but I try my luck anyway with the afternoon crowd.

"Hey, have you guys heard about Hank Easton?" I ask, trying to sound casual. "He used to work out here in the morning."

One of the women looks up and smiles. "I've probably seen him go once or twice before. Why?"

"I'm trying to piece together what happened to him," I say, lowering my voice. "Did any of you ever see him with a woman? Possibly around 5'3" to 5'6"?"

They exchange glances, and one of the men nods slowly. "You're going to have to provide a better description than that. That describes more than half of the female population right?" The others chuckle in unison.

"Not technically. Half the population doesn't frequent this gym. So I'd only be referring to women who possibly meet the description in this gym."

"Again, that's many people. We didn't know the guy enough to be bothered with who he associates with. Are you a cop?"

"I'm not but thank you anyway." I hear the soft murmur of whispers as I walk away. I linger a bit at the gym to not raise any suspicion by abruptly leaving. I walk the treadmill, absentmindedly, eagerly awaiting the response to my Shadow Stalker update from the local police.

CHAPTER 20
CARTER

Back at the precinct, everything feels off. The usual hum of activity seems tinged with an undercurrent of tension. I can feel the change in the air, like the calm before a storm. The news from the Shadow Stalker page has thrown everyone for a loop, and it's all anyone can talk about. The suspect is likely a woman. I've known this for a while, but I kept it to myself, playing my cards close to my chest. Now, that secret is out, the reaction is palpable.

I find out about the update through my colleagues, who are buzzing with the news. Some of them are careful around me, not sharing too much since Booker has advised them to keep things close. Booker and I have always had a contentious relationship, but now it's more pronounced. She's made it clear that she doesn't want me involved in the case anymore.

But then there's Harper, who's now working alongside Booker. She doesn't seem too happy about the change, and she makes sure to keep me in the loop. It's around lunchtime when she suggests we grab a bite at a local deli, away from prying ears.

We walk to Louie's Deli, a small place with checkered tablecloths and the best pastrami sandwiches in town. As we settle into a corner booth, Harper looks around to make sure no one from the precinct is nearby. "I'm really not taking to Booker," she says, her voice low but filled with frustration. "She's rude and standoffish. It's like she thinks she's above everyone."

I agree, taking a bite of my sandwich. "That sounds like Booker. What's the latest?"

"She's shifting the department's focus to finding a woman. The problem is, she couldn't get the footage from Hank Easton's neighbor. The description we have is vague at best."

I feel a mix of satisfaction and frustration. Satisfaction that Booker is struggling, but frustration because it's still a step in the right direction for her. "What did the neighbor say exactly?"

Harper leans in closer. "He described the figure as a woman, dressed in black, between 5'3" and 5'6". She entered Hank's yard but there's no footage of her leaving. He said a detective said it was okay to delete the footage after a quick review, which seems odd." My stomach churns. He's referring to our encounter. I hadn't explicitly told him to delete the footage but when he asked if he needed to maintain it I advised him that it wasn't necessary. Fully aware of the complications that might arise or consequences that might take place as a result of this being discovered.

Our meeting was off the books. I'd never given the department a reason not to trust me so if it comes down to it, I could deny it. It'd be his words against mine. Or it would be regarded as a misunderstanding. I could explain that I didn't share the details because the footage was no good. Too far, too grainy and unclear. It would not help us in identifying a particular suspect in the case.

His conclusion that it was a woman was merely an assumption. The figure mimics that of a typical woman but it could be anyone. I frown. "That is odd.." I say keeping my response short.

"Exactly," Harper says, shaking her head. "Anyway, I don't trust her judgment. But I'll keep you posted on any new updates." We finish our lunch, the conversation drifting to lighter topics for a bit, but my mind keeps returning to the case. As we walk back to the precinct, Harper gives me a reassuring pat on the back.

"We'll figure this out, Carter. Booker or no Booker." I smile, appreciating her loyalty. "Thanks, Harper. I'll need all the help I can get."

At home, Phoebe is waiting for me. She looks up from her book as I walk in. "How was your day?" she asks. I sigh, dropping my jacket on the couch. I explain to her that Booker is making it hard on me back at the office. She's barred the team from sharing confidential case details.

"We're all certain the Shadow Stalker is a woman. To the department, that's a big break in the case. Bigger than anything I've uncovered."

"I'm sorry hun."

"It's okay. It's all my fault. But I found something. One of Jacob Garcia's victims, Channing Reid, is very vocal about his past. He runs a support group, and there was a meeting the other night. I went, but I didn't go inside. I need to talk to him alone."

Phoebe frowns. "Do you think he knows something?"

"Maybe. He's been posting a lot about Garcia's death, calling it karma. It's worth a shot."

She nods, her expression serious. "Be careful. This

is dangerous territory."

"I know," I say, sitting down beside her. "But I have to do something. I can't just sit back and let Booker take over."

Phoebe takes my hand, squeezing it gently. "I believe in you. Just promise me you'll be careful."

"I promise," I say, leaning in to kiss her.

Later in bed, I can't sleep. I lie staring at the ceiling, my mind running through everything I've learned. The scene of the meeting returns to me. What was *she* doing there? How is *she* connected to the members?

The next morning, I decide to pay another visit to the community center, hoping to catch Channing alone. I arrive early, parking in the same spot as before. The building is quiet, and I wait, watching the entrance. A few minutes later, I see Channing arrive. He's a tall, lean man with a determined look in his eyes. He glances around before heading inside, and I take the opportunity to follow him.

Inside, the building is quiet, just the faint hum of fluorescent lights overhead. I find the meeting room again and wait outside, listening for any sounds. After a few minutes, the door opens, and Channing steps out. He looks startled when he sees me, but quickly composes himself.

"Sir, can I help you?" he asks, his tone wary.

I step forward, holding out my hand. "Detective Carter. I'm investigating the recent murders, including Jacob Garcia's. I'd like to ask you a few questions."

Channing hesitates, then nods, forming a slight grin on his face while shaking my hand. "It's about time. Let's talk outside." We step out into the cold, and he leads me to a bench near the side of the building. He sits down, looking at me expectantly before pulling a pack of cigarettes from his jacket. He gestures to offer me one and I politely decline. He sparks one up without bothering to ask if I mind.

"Well, what do you want to know?" he asks, letting out a puff.

"I've been looking into the connections between the victims," I say, choosing my words carefully. "I noticed you've been very vocal about Jacob Garcia and his past. Can you tell me more about your experience with him?"

Channing's expression hardens. "Jacob was a monster. He assaulted me, along with several others. We came forward, but he got off with a slap on the wrist. It was infuriating. He had a great lawyer, and we didn't stand a chance."

I nod, understanding his anger. "I saw your posts about his death. You called it karma. Do you have any idea who might have done it?"

Channing shakes his head. "No, but I'm not surprised. He had a lot of enemies, people he hurt. It was only a matter of time before someone decided to take matters into their own hands." He shrugs.

I study him, trying to gauge if he's hiding something. "What about the other victims? Gary Robinson, Hank Easton, Daniel Edwards, Liam Harris. Do you know anything about them?"

He frowns, thinking. "I've only heard of them through what's published in the news."

"Do you think it could be someone from your support group?" I ask.

Channing looks surprised. He makes no effort to hide his irritation as he sucks his teeth and rolls his eyes. "Listen honey, Jacob had it coming. He probably crawled in bed with the wrong person. I'm not totally convinced his murder had anything to do with the other's. Unless you know something I don't. No one here would want him dead but me and I wouldn't be sitting here casually talking to you if I was guilty."

He crosses his arms and throws one leg over the other, brow furrowed as if he is waiting on answers. I pause as I realize that I may have inadvertently revealed too much information that has not yet been made public by the department. The community isn't aware that the suspect is targeting sexual offenders. "I just thought that there's a possibility that a supporter may have become too passionate about the topics shared between those walls."

He shakes his head. "Well, they'd be my hero," he chuckles. "But no one here raises any concerns. I'll keep my ears open. If I hear anything, I'll let you know."

"Thank you," I say, standing up. "I appreciate your help."

"Good luck, Detective. I hope you find whoever's doing this. Truly."

CHAPTER 21
AILA

I lie on the loveseat in my living room, eyes glued to the television as the local police department hosts a press update. The new detective leading the case, Detective Booker, stands at the podium, her expression serious as she begins the briefing. "We have new information regarding the Shadow Stalker," she announces, "We believe the suspect to be a woman."

The room buzzes with murmurs and questions from the press. One reporter stands up, microphone in hand. "Can you provide a description of the suspect?" Booker takes a moment before answering.

"The description is not yet clear. For now, we're looking for a woman between 5'3" and 5'6"." The crowd erupts in dissatisfaction.

"That's a weak description!" someone shouts. "You must have nothing."

"How long have you known this information?" another voice demands. Booker remains composed, but I can see the strain in her eyes. I turn off the TV, feeling annoyed. This case is becoming a tangled web of misinformation and dead ends, and I'm starting to realize that if anyone is going to get to the bottom of it, it won't be Rutledge PD. It's like they are following my lead.

I decide to dig deeper into the background of the fifth victim, Gary Robinson. I head back to the sports lounge where he worked, hoping to find some answers. The place is lively with the evening crowd, but I'm focused on my task. I approach the bar and ask to speak with one of Gary's former coworkers. "I'm looking into Gary Robinson's background. Can you tell me anything about him?"

The bartender, a young woman with dark hair and tired eyes, nods slowly. "What do you want to know? We've told you guys what we know. The story hasn't changed. He was a questionable guy. Did his job well but often straddled the lines of appropriate versus inappropriate behavior. He was reported twice, and honestly, I think he would have been fired soon."

"I'm honestly looking for more information into his past," I say, trying to sound casual.

"None of us really knew him outside of work."

"What about the owner?"

"What about him? Gary, like the rest of us, was hired during a job fair for the lounge. When we first opened, the owner was pretty much hiring on the spot. Since the hiring process concluded, we don't see much of him. I doubt he has or had anything to do with Gary personally."

"Had Gary ever made you feel uncomfortable?"

"If second-hand discomfort counts," she pauses, "but no, not personally."

"Can I give you my cell? If you hear anything else, would you be willing to follow up with me."

"Sure. I can't make any promises."

"No need." I smile slightly and head for the exit.

Gary's problematic behavior is not the concrete evidence I'm searching for. My phone buzzes with a notification from Echo. I glance at the screen and see a message from what appears to be a phony page. The profile has no real photos, only graphics and minimal updates. Curious, I open the message. It reads:

Hello friend, I saw your posts about Gary and thought I could share my experience. I'm from Bentley, IL, just like Gary. We met after I left a bar and got into a rideshare car driven by him. I had too many drinks that night. My destination was my dorm, but Gary took a detour. That prompt change snapped me out of my drunken haze as fear set in. I asked where he was going, and he pulled over into a dark alley off the main road, telling me to calm down. He lied, saying he got lost and needed to reset his GPS. He looked at me through the rearview mirror in a way that made my skin crawl. When I tried to open the door to get out, I found the child lock activated. Gary began to climb into the backseat, and I fought and screamed. Thankfully, someone nearby heard the commotion and knocked on the window, forcing Gary to retreat to the front and unlock the doors. He feigned confusion, saying I was drunk and having an outburst, claiming I'd asked him to pull over to vomit. I reported him to the rideshare app, but I'm not sure what came of it. I hope everything gets resolved over in Rutledge.

As I pull up to my apartment, I notice an unfamiliar car parked in front. My heart sinks when I see who's sitting in the driver's seat. It's my mom, looking as glamorous as ever. She's come all the way from New York, and this is the absolute worst possible time for a surprise visit. I'm knee-deep in this case, trying to piece together the mystery of the Shadow Stalker, and I don't have the bandwidth for anything else right now.

I take a deep breath and get out of my car, walking over to her. She steps out of her car, her face lighting up when she sees me. She's wearing a fitted, emerald green jumpsuit that accentuates her tall, slender frame while a Tian Zevon clutch glistens from her hand. Her auburn hair is perfectly styled, cascading in waves over her shoulders, and her makeup is flawless, as always. Her clog booties clamp against the pavement as she walks over to me, enveloping me in a hug.

"Hi darling! It's so good to see you!" she exclaims, her voice warm but with that hint of underlying scrutiny that I know so well.

"Mom, what a surprise," I say, trying to match her enthusiasm but feeling the weight of my day pressing down on me. "What brings you here?"

"I have a twelve-hour layover on my way to the West Coast, and I thought it would be rude not to drop by and see my daughter," she says with a wink. I unlock and swing my door open inviting her inside. She scans the small space before taking a seat on the sofa. "How have you been?"

I manage a smile, though it feels strained. "I've been good. Just busy with work, you know."

She raises an eyebrow. "Oh, really? What kind of work are you doing these days?"

I pause, careful not to mention anything about the case. "Just the usual, Mom. Nothing too exciting."

"Hmm," she says, clearly not buying it. "And how's Jaison? You two doing well?"

"Yeah, we're good. He's been busy with his work,

but we're managing," I say.

She sighs, her expression softening. "Honey, you know I just had my birthday, right?"

My stomach churns as I feel a twinge of guilt. "Mom, I'm so sorry I forgot. I've just been so swamped lately."

She waves her hand dismissively. "You forget every year, sweetheart. I'm used to it by now."

"Still, I should have remembered."

"Well, it's in the past now." I offer her tea and head to the kitchen to start it. She follows me, leaning against the counter as she watches me.

"So, how's everything with Dr. Gore and... you know... your health." I turn to face her, trying to keep my expression neutral.

"I'm fine, Mom. Just a bit stressed with work, but that's normal."

"Are you sure? You always say you're fine, but I worry about you," she says, her eyes searching mine.

"I promise, I'm okay.".

She nods slowly, but I can tell she's not entirely convinced. She takes the cup of tea that I pour and stirs in one spoon of sugar. "I told your dad I'd ask about children. It's no rush. It's just... you're fixing to be thirty. You know I had you when I was twenty-one. So, I guess I expected a grandbaby by now."

My stomach tightens at the question. I've always had mixed feelings about having children. The thought of exposing them to genetic misfortunes, given my family's history, terrifies me. And with Jaison and me both so engrossed in our work, we're not in a position to dedicate a lot of time to a child right now.

"Mom, Jaison and I have talked about it, but we're

just not ready yet. We're both really focused on our work, and we don't want to bring a child into the world unless we can give them the time and attention they deserve."

She looks at me for a long moment before walking off. "I understand. I just want you to be happy and I worry that you're putting off things that are important."

"I know, Mom. I appreciate your concern. But we're just not there yet," I say, joining her in the living room.

I feel a wave of relief wash over me knowing she'll be gone by the morning. Time passes in a blur of small talk and catching up. My mind keeps drifting back to the case, but I do my best to stay present. Naturally, the conversation drifts to the Shadow Stalker news and I deny having any details and assure her that Jaison and I are making extra efforts to make sure we stay safe.

When Jaison arrives home, my mom immediately gravitates towards him, as she always does. Ever since they met, she's been incredibly fond of him, practically adopting him as her own son. She peppers him with questions, asking about his well-being, his job, and how he's handling everything. It's a barrage of maternal concern that I'm used to, but today it feels especially suffocating.

Despite our earlier conversation, she can't resist bringing up the topic of children again. "So, Jaison, when are you two going to give me a grandchild?" she asks, her eyes twinkling with anticipation. I brace myself for the familiar response, the one we've rehearsed and agreed upon. But to my shock, Jaison replies, "I'm ready whenever she is."

I shoot him a sharp look, my eyes wide with surprise and a hint of panic. That's not the story we've agreed on. He meets my gaze and realizes his mistake, but the damage is already done. My mom's face lights up.

"Really, Jaison? That's wonderful to hear!" She turns to me, clearly delighted. "See? He's ready. What's holding you back?" I try to hide my frustration and force a smile. She waves her hand dismissively. To divert the conversation, she heads to the kitchen and fixes Jaison a plate of leftovers from our earlier meal. I follow them to the living room, trying to shake off the unease that her visit has stirred up.

We settle on the couch and continue our conversation. My mom asks Jaison about his day, his projects at work, and even throws in some light-hearted banter about sports, which she knows nothing about but pretends to, just to connect with him. Jaison, always the diplomat, engages with her warmly, making her laugh and feel included.

As the evening wears on, I find myself zoning out. Eventually, the conversation winds down. My mom looks at the clock and stands up, stretching. "I should get some rest. Early flight tomorrow," she says, giving us both a tired but contented smile.

"Of course, Mom," I say, standing up to hug her. "Safe travels, and thanks for stopping by."

She hugs me tightly, then turns to Jaison, giving him a warm embrace as well. "Take care of my girl, Jaison. And don't let her work too hard."

He chuckles, "I'll do my best." After she leaves, I let out a long sigh of relief. The apartment feels quieter, almost too quiet now. I glance at Jaison, who looks sheepish. "Sorry about earlier," he says, scratching the back of his head. "I didn't mean to put you on the spot."

"It's fine," I say, though I know it's not. "We just need to be on the same page next time."

"Agreed." We tidy up the living room in silence, each of us lost in our own thoughts. As we finally head to bed, I can't shake the feeling of unease. My mom's visit has stirred up more than just family drama—it's reminded me of the ticking clock and the pressure I'm under to solve this case and get back to family. I just hope I can keep everything from falling apart.

CHAPTER 22
CARTER

I dig into a bowl of ramen I picked up from the restaurant down the street. The steam wafts up, carrying the savory aroma that usually makes my mouth water, but today it's hard to focus on anything other than the mess work has become. My desk is cluttered with files and papers scattered haphazardly. I take a sip of the broth, hoping it will soothe the knot in my stomach.

I'm startled by a sharp knock on my door and I look up to see Detective Booker standing there, her face set in a stern expression. "Carter, can I speak with you for a moment?" she asks, her tone leaving little room for refusal. I consider telling her I'm too busy, especially since I'm no longer on her case and don't have to answer to her. But something in her eyes tells me she won't take no for an answer.

"Fine," I say, setting my chopsticks down with a sigh. "What do you need, Booker?"

She steps into my office, closing the door behind her. "I need to talk to you about the neighbor of Hank Easton," she begins.

I raise an eyebrow, playing it cool. "What about

him?"

"After the Shadow Stalker page updated about the suspect appearing to be a woman on the surveillance footage from the neighbor's house, I have some questions," she says, narrowing her eyes at me. "When exactly did you meet with this neighbor?"

I lean back in my chair, trying to appear nonchalant. "I met with him briefly," I reply, keeping my voice steady.

"And why didn't you share the news of the suspect being a woman?" she presses, crossing her arms over her chest.

I take a deep breath, choosing my words carefully. "I personally reviewed the footage," I say slowly. "It was too grainy, and the subject was too far away. There was no way to tell the gender of the suspect. In a high-stakes case like this, there's no room for assumptions. You get something so vital wrong, and it could tank the entire case." Booker doesn't look convinced.

"Then why withhold the details from the team?"

"Reviewing the footage had no bearing on progressing the case because nothing could be seen besides a figure entering the yard," I say, hoping she buys my explanation. Anticipating her next question, I add, "I advised the neighbor to hold onto the footage just in case it might serve a purpose in the future, which, frankly, I didn't think it would."

She scowls, clearly not satisfied with my answers. "If I find out you've been obstructing evidence and jeopardizing this case, I will enjoy taking you down," she warns. "I'm starting from the top and investigating the case from the beginning. I will get to the bottom of everything."

I stand up, feeling the tension radiate through my

body. "Do what you have to do," I say, walking over to the door and opening it wide. "But you can start by leaving my office." She glares at me for a moment before storming out. I close the door behind her, the sound echoing in the silence of my office. I return to my desk and sit down heavily, my appetite completely gone.

Booker is digging, and I know I need to be careful. The stakes are higher than ever, and one wrong move could bring everything crashing down. I take a deep breath and try to refocus, but it's hard to shake the feeling that the walls are closing in. I find it difficult to concentrate. My mind keeps racing, replaying our conversation. I know she's determined to unravel this case, and I can't afford any slip-ups. I look at the clock and realize I've been sitting here for over an hour, lost in thought.

I shift my energy to the cases I've been assigned. They are low-profile, mundane, and far from the intensity of the Shadow Stalker investigation. The first file I open is about a series of petty thefts in a quiet suburban neighborhood. Lawn ornaments, garden tools, and even a lawnmower have gone missing. I sigh, rubbing my temples. It's not that these cases aren't important to the people involved, but they lack the adrenaline and urgency of the investigations I'm used to. If this is the captain's way of punishing me for grossly mishandling the case, the message is clear. It's almost like I've been demoted to patrol.

I grab my notepad and head out. As I walk through the precinct, I catch snippets of conversations. I can feel eyes on me, whispers following my steps. Booker must have already spread the word about her intentions. I need to be careful. I drive to the neighborhood. The sun is shining, birds are chirping, and it's hard to imagine anything sinister happening here. I talk to a few of the residents, jotting down notes as they describe their missing items. One resident is particularly upset about her missing gnome collection.

"I just don't understand why anyone would take them," she says, her voice quivering.

"I'll do my best to find them."

Next, I visit the local hardware store where the owner reports that someone has been stealing small items. He's an older man, his white hair thinning, and he looks at me with a mixture of hope and skepticism.

"Do you think you'll catch whoever's doing this?" he asks, leaning on the counter.

"I'll try," I say, managing a weak smile. "But it might take some time."

The next case is a noise complaint. Neighbors are arguing over a loud party that happened over the weekend. I drive to the neighborhood, where the houses are neatly lined up, identical lawns manicured to perfection. The complainant meets me at the door. She's an older woman with a stern expression, her arms crossed over her chest.

"It was absolutely outrageous," she says, shaking her head. "The noise went on until three in the morning."

I nod, taking notes. "Did you call the police at the time?"

"Of course I did," she snaps. "But by the time they arrived, the noise had stopped." I speak to a few more neighbors, all of whom echo her sentiments. They're tired of the disturbances, and they want something done about it. I assure them I'll file a report and speak to the party's host. It's the same story, just a different neighborhood.

This isn't what I signed up for. I joined the force to make a difference, to solve crimes that matter. Yet here I am, chasing down garden gnome thieves and hardware store crooks. Back at the precinct, I write up my reports.

The details are dull, and I struggle to keep my eyes from glazing over as I type. The rhythm of the keys tapping is almost hypnotic.

Midway through my report, my phone buzzes. It's a text from Jenkins:

Booker is on a warpath today. Be careful.

I shake my head, a bitter laugh escaping my lips. Of course she is. Booker's relentless, and I know she's itching to find any reason to make my life harder. I shove my phone back into my pocket and focus on finishing my report. The cases blur together, a monotonous parade of minor issues. Harper thumps her finger against my door which is half open.

"How's it going?" she asks, leaning against the doorframe.

I shrug. "Same old. Petty thefts, noise complaints. Nothing exciting."

She gives me a sympathetic look. "I heard Booker's really pushing hard on the case."

"Yeah," I mutter, turning back to my computer. "She's determined to make me look bad."

Harper steps into the office, closing the door behind her. "Just hang in there, Carter. Don't let her get to you."

"Thanks, Harper. I'll try."

She offers to bring me a drink from the vending machine, sealed. I thank her but decline and explain that I am heading out soon. When I finally shut down my computer and grab my coat, it's late, and the precinct is nearly empty. I take the long route home, allowing myself the time to think and plan my next move without interruption. Booker's not going to back down, and I need to be ready for whatever comes next. The case has taken on a life of its own, and I'm determined to see it through, no matter the cost.

CHAPTER 23
AILA

Finally, my appointment time arrives. I drive to Dr. Gore's office, my stomach in knots. The familiar building looms ahead, and I take a moment to steady myself before walking inside. The waiting room is quiet, with soft music playing in the background. I check in at the front desk and take a seat, my mind racing with thoughts of what I might say.

After a few minutes, Dr. Gore appears in the doorway, a warm smile on his face. "Aila, it's good to see you," he says, gesturing for me to follow him to his office. I stand up, smoothing down my clothes, and walk into his office.

"It's good to see you too, Dr. Gore," I reply, trying to sound more confident than I feel.

We sit down in his cozy office, filled with books and calming artwork. The atmosphere is soothing, and I feel a small sense of comfort returning.

Dr. Gore sits across from me, his notepad in hand. "How have you been, Aila?" he asks.

I force a smile. "I've been okay, I guess. Busy." I take a deep breath and begin to explain everything—the case, the nightmares, the anxiety that's been building up inside me.

"You mentioned that you've been having nightmares again. Do you want to talk about them?"

"They're always the same. I'm being hunted by the same figure. I can never get a clear image of the face. Just when I am about to be attacked, each time, I wake up."

Dr. Gore listens intently, his eyes never leaving mine. "That sounds terrifying, Aila. Have you noticed if these nightmares are more frequent when you're stressed?"

I nod. "Yeah, they definitely get worse when I'm stressed."

He leans back in his chair, considering my words. "I know the Shadow Stalker case has been all over the news lately. Do you think that could be contributing to your anxiety?"

I hesitate, not wanting to reveal how closely I've been following the case. "Maybe. It's hard not to think about it when it's everywhere."

Dr. Gore nods thoughtfully. "It's understandable. The media coverage can be overwhelming. How have you been managing your stress?"

I shrug. "I try to stay busy. I go for runs, I spend time with Jaison. But it doesn't always help."

He makes another note. "What about your medication? Have you been taking it consistently?"

I feel a pang of guilt. "Yes," I lie, forcing myself to meet his gaze.

Dr. Gore's eyes search mine for a moment before he nods. "Good. It's important to stay on top of that. Have you been doing the breathing exercises we talked about?"

I nod again, this time truthfully. "Yes, those do help sometimes."

He smiles. "That's great to hear. Remember, it's all about finding what works best for you. Consistency is key."

There's a brief silence as he writes down more notes, and I take the opportunity to gather my thoughts. Dr. Gore has helped me through some of my darkest times. But there's something about today's session that feels different, more intense.

"Aila," he says, breaking the silence. "Have you talked to Hunter or Didi recently?"

My heart skips a beat at the mention of their names. "No," I say quietly. "I haven't been in touch with either of them."

He looks at me with concern. "What about the others?"

"No, not them either."

His expression becomes unreadable. "I see. It's important to stay connected with the people who support you. Isolation can make everything feel more overwhelming."

I know he's right, but the thought of reaching out to Hunter, DiDi, or any of the others feels impossible right now. "I'll try," I say, though I'm not sure I mean it.

Dr. Gore smiles gently. "That's all I can ask. Just take it one step at a time."

As the session continues, we talk about different strategies to manage my stress and anxiety. Dr. Gore suggests a few new techniques, like mindfulness meditation and keeping a journal of my thoughts and feelings. He also reminds me to stay active and maintain a routine, even when things feel chaotic. Eventually, the session comes to an end. I thank Dr. Gore and leave his office, feeling exhausted.

I consider reconnecting with Hunter and DiDi, old friends of mine. Perhaps what I need are great friends to pull my mind away from the very things that threaten to destroy me. I quickly push the thought to the back of my head. Hunter, DiDi, and the others were no good for me. With them, I found myself in a mountain of trouble. I made riskier decisions and some that almost cost me my marriage. I made a vow to myself and Jaison that I could learn to stick to myself and those who bring peace. Dr. Gore knows about some of my experiences with them but not all. So, I know that his suggestion comes from a good place. In the end, I also don't need too many distractions from solving the nightmares and bringing peace back to Rutledge.

The morning light filters through the blinds, casting faint patterns on the wall. I sit up in bed, my mind still heavy with the remnants of yesterday's conversation with Dr. Gore. The thought of returning to that chaotic part of my life is too risky. I can't afford to let my guard down. I get up and head to the kitchen, where Jaison is already making coffee. He smiles when he sees me, a reassuring sight amidst my turmoil. "Morning, babe," he says, handing me a steaming mug.

"Morning," I reply, taking a sip. The warmth spreads through me, momentarily easing my nervousness.

"Did you sleep well?" he asks, his concern genuine.

I nod, not wanting to burden him with the truth. "Better than usual," I lie, offering a small smile.

We talk about mundane things—his work, our plans for the weekend. I know I must talk to him about the conversation that I had with Gore and how it made me feel but now's not the time. I prepare him a quick lunch to take with him to work. I head to the Anchor, for a round of drinks.

CHAPTER 24
CARTER

I arrive at the bakery a little earlier than planned, the sweet aroma of fresh donuts and muffins greets me at the door. Jenkins and Harper are already there, sitting at a corner table. Harper is laughing at something Jenkins said.

"Morning," I say, sliding into the seat next to Jenkins. "What's so funny?"

Harper grins, her eyes twinkling mischievously. "Just Jenkins trying to remember the last time he successfully parallel parked. It's a miracle he hasn't lost his license yet."

Jenkins rolls his eyes, but a smile tugs at the corner of his lips. "I'm a great driver. It's just the parking that gets me."

We laugh and start digging into the box of donuts between us. I go for a classic glazed, appreciating the sugary goodness as I take a bite.

"So," Harper says, wiping powdered sugar from her lips, "how are you, Carter? We've heard Booker's been a real piece of work."

I sigh, leaning back in my chair. "She's been on a power trip since she got her promotion."

Jenkins nods, his expression serious. "Some of the detectives don't trust her judgment. Others just flat-out don't like her. She's drawing a wedge between the team."

Harper's grin turns wicked. "You know, one of these days, I might just slip a little something into her coffee. Nothing deadly, just enough to give her a scare."

I don't find the joke funny and my face must show it. She laughs, but there's a hint of nervousness in her eyes. "I was only kidding. Mostly."

Jenkins changes the subject. "Any updates on your end, Carter?"

I shake my head. "Nothing's changed. I've been stuck on these low-profile cases, and it's pure torture. It's like they want to keep me busy with meaningless work."

Harper and Jenkins exchange sympathetic looks. "That sucks, man," Jenkins says. We finish our donuts and coffee, the mood a little more subdued now. We walk to the precinct and when we arrive, Booker is waiting for me in my office. The sight of her there, standing with that self-righteous expression, makes my blood boil. I take a deep breath and brace myself for whatever fresh hell she's about to unleash.

"Carter," she says, her tone cold and professional, "we need to talk."

I force a smile, though it feels more like a grimace. "What is it now, Booker?"

She steps closer, her eyes locking onto mine. "I backtracked like I said I would. Went by Liam Harris' apartment building again. A woman who frequents the area spoke with me—a homeless lady. She says she saw a suspicious woman, around the time of the murder, lurking around the building, prying."

I fold my arms across my chest, keeping my voice

steady. "Go on."

"A woman in her mid-twenties, honey blonde hair, hazel eyes, wearing an expensive ring on her finger. Sound familiar?" I follow Booker's gaze as it shifts to the photo on my desk, the one of Phoebe. I can see her scanning Phoebe's face, attempting to make connections.

My heart skips a beat, but I keep my expression neutral. "You think this has something to do with me?"

Booker's eyes narrow. "I think it's all starting to make sense. Why you've made no progress in this case, why you've been working off the books and manipulating findings. I believe you're protecting someone, Carter. Someone close to you."

I laugh, though there's no humor in it. "You're grasping at straws, Booker. You're under pressure to solve this case, and you're making wild accusations. If this is the best you've got, then you're the worst detective this precinct has ever seen."

Her face hardens, but she doesn't back down. "If I find out you've been obstructing this investigation, I will take you down. Mark my words."

I feel a surge of anger and disbelief. "Are you seriously accusing me of working with Phoebe? You think we're behind the Shadow Stalker updates? That we're some kind of vigilante duo?"

Booker's eyes flash. "I believe Phoebe is running that page and you're helping her cover her tracks. Together, you're murdering people with questionable pasts."

My patience has worn thin. "You're insane, Booker. Stop harassing me, or you'll be back on a desk when I report you. Get out of my office. Now."

She doesn't move immediately, holding my gaze for a long moment before finally turning on her heel to storm out, slamming the door behind her. The moment she's gone, I feel the weight of the situation settles. I have to get out of here. I grab my coat and decide to go home early

When I get home, the silence is deafening. I pace the living room, my mind racing. Booker is getting too close. The accusations she's throwing around are dangerous, and I don't know how to stop her without making things worse.

Phoebe arrives shortly after, a look of concern on her face as she sees me pacing. "What's wrong?"

"Booker suspects you," I say, my voice strained. "She thinks we're working together, that you're behind the Shadow Stalker updates and we're murdering people."

Phoebe's eyes widen. "That's absurd! On what basis?"

I explain everything Booker said, watching as Phoebe's face shifts from shock to anger. "This is ridiculous. I'll go down to the station right now and clear my name."

"No," I say firmly. "It's just Booker. She doesn't have any hardcore evidence, and she hasn't brought the department in on this yet. You need to stay away from the station. Let me handle this."

Phoebe looks at me, her eyes searching mine. "Are you sure?"

"I'll take care of it. But you need to brace yourself, just in case. This isn't going to be easy."

She sighs, sinking onto the couch. "I can't believe this is happening."

I sit beside her, taking her hand. "Don't get yourself worked up. It'll all be okay."

The rest of the evening passes in a blur. I try to keep

my mind occupied, but it's impossible to shake the feeling of dread that's settled in my chest. I need to find a way to prove Booker wrong, to show that Phoebe and I are innocent. But I also know that every move I make could be scrutinized, and one wrong step could make things worse.

The night is still when I slip out of my apartment as the city is cloaked in shadows. I drive with the headlights off, taking back roads to avoid any late-night traffic or nosy neighbors who might be up. The streets are empty, just the way I like it. The cool night air seeps through the car's open window, keeping me alert as I navigate the quiet roads to Booker's neighborhood.

I park a few blocks away, in a spot where the streetlamp has been out for weeks. It's dark enough to conceal my car but not so dark that it would draw suspicion. Stepping out, I close the door softly, my footsteps nearly silent as I walk toward her house. The neighborhood is decent, filled with modest homes, each one a little different from the next but all maintaining a sense of order.

Booker's house is at the end of the street, a single-story home with a well-kept yard and a white picket fence. It looks like something out of a suburban dream, but I know better. It's a facade, much like the woman herself. I stick to the shadows, moving along the fence line until I reach her backyard. The bushes here are thick, providing ample coverage as I settle in to watch.

Through the window, I see her sitting at the kitchen counter. She's wearing reading glasses, a sight I've never seen before. It makes her look almost human, a stark contrast to the iron-fisted superior she is at the precinct. A mug steams in her hand as she reads something intently. The soft glow of the kitchen light casts a warm hue over the scene, making it almost domestic. I can see the concentration on her face, the slight furrow in her brow as she focuses on the text in front of her.

She lives alone, as I suspected. There's no sign of pets, no barking dog or creeping cat to give away my presence. No cars pass by, no voices drift from the nearby houses. It's just me and the rhythmic sound of crickets in the distance. I scan the neighboring houses. Most windows are dark, curtains drawn for the night. One house has a porch light on, but it's dim and flickers occasionally. It's almost as if the entire neighborhood is holding its breath, waiting for something to happen.

I crouch lower in the bushes, my legs starting to cramp from the awkward position, but I stay put. This is my only chance to learn her routine, to figure out if she has any vulnerabilities I can exploit. She turns a page, sips her drink, and I wonder what she's reading. Something work-related, no doubt. Booker doesn't strike me as the type to indulge in light fiction or magazines.

My mind races with thoughts of what I'm doing and why. This isn't just about staying ahead of her investigation. It's about survival. If she discovers the truth, it could ruin everything. My career, my life—it all hangs in the balance. Watching her now, seeing the ordinary way she conducts herself, almost makes me doubt my fears. But I can't afford to take chances.

A light turns on in one of the neighboring houses, catching my attention. I hold my breath, waiting to see if anyone steps outside or looks my way, but the light flicks off just as quickly as it came on. Probably someone getting a late-night drink or using the bathroom. Still, it reminds me of the risk I'm taking. One misstep, one curious neighbor, and I could be exposed.

Booker closes her book, removing her glasses and rubbing her eyes. She looks tired, worn out from the day. I almost feel a pang of sympathy for her. Almost. But then I remember her threats, the way she's hounding me, and the sympathy evaporates. She stands up, stretching before heading towards what I assume is her bedroom. The kitchen light stays on, casting long shadows that dance across the room as she moves.

I stay in my hiding spot, waiting until I'm sure she's settled in for the night. The last thing I need is for her to catch me lurking outside her window. Finally, after what feels like an hour, the lights in the house go out one by one. I wait a bit longer, listening for any sounds but the house remains silent. Carefully, I retrace my steps, sticking to the shadows as I make my way back to the car. The street is still empty. I slip into the driver's seat and start the engine, keeping the lights off until I'm a safe distance away.

Back home, I lie in bed, staring at the ceiling. Booker is alone, vulnerable in ways she doesn't realize. If I play my cards right, I can stay one step ahead of her. I can protect Phoebe, protect myself. But I have to be careful. As I drift off to sleep, the image of Booker sitting at her counter with those reading glasses lingers in my mind. She's not invincible, and neither am I. But for now, the game continues.

CHAPTER 25
AILA

The air feels thick as I sit in the waiting room of Dr. Gore's office. I glance around, taking in the sterile white walls and framed motivational posters that I've seen a hundred times before. The faint hum of the fluorescent lights adds to my anxiety, a constant reminder that I'm here because I'm not okay. I fidget in my seat, twisting the strap of my bag between my fingers, trying to calm the storm inside me.

"Aila, Dr. Gore will see you now," the receptionist calls out, her voice soft as it cuts through my chaotic thoughts. The short walk to his office feels like a mile. When I push open the door, he's there, sitting behind his desk with a warm, reassuring smile on his face.

"Come in. Please, have a seat," he says, gesturing to the comfortable chair opposite his desk.

I slump into the chair, my body tense and my mind whirring with everything I need to say. He waits patiently with his hands folded on the desk, giving me the space to gather my thoughts.

"Dr. Gore, I... I don't know where to start," I finally manage to say with a shaky voice.

"Take your time. There's no rush," he replies.

I take another deep breath, trying to steady myself. "Hunter reached out to me. He said he's been trying to contact me for a while now. I don't know why this is freaking me out so much, but it is."

Dr. Gore nods, "Let's take a step back. Why do you think you're uncomfortable reconnecting with Hunter?"

I bite my lip, feeling a mix of emotions surge through me. "Our relationship has caused so much turmoil in my life. He was there for me when I was younger, after... after the accident that landed me in the hospital. I don't remember much of my life before that, but Hunter was like a guardian to me at first. He helped me cope with all the changes."

Dr. Gore leans forward slightly, his eyes full of understanding. "Can you tell me more about how you met Hunter and what your relationship was like?"

My hands tremble as I clasp them together. "I met Hunter when I was 16. I don't remember much from before that age because of the accident. It was a tragic event, and I was in the hospital for two weeks. I met him there. Hunter was there for me during that time. He protected me, nurtured me, and helped me adapt to the new reality I found myself in."

"That must have been a very challenging time for you," Dr. Gore says softly.

"It was," I admit, my voice barely above a whisper. "At first, having Hunter around was a good thing. He made me feel safe. But then things changed. He started trying to pressure me into doing dangerous and illegal things, like living on the edge was the only way to feel alive. That's when I began to pull away from him."

Dr. Gore listens intently, his expression encouraging me to continue.

"Didi was always close to Hunter," I continue. "She encouraged his behavior. I met her through him, and she was just as reckless. Being around them felt like walking a tightrope. Eventually, I realized I needed to let them go if I wanted to make any progress in my life."

He takes a moment, considering my words. "It sounds like Hunter and Didi were significant figures in your life during a very formative time. Letting them go was likely a necessary step for your growth and well-being. It's understandable that reconnecting with Hunter now brings up a lot of conflicting emotions."

I agree, feeling a lump form in my throat. "I know he's reaching out, but I don't want to go back to that life. It feels like I've worked so hard to move forward."

"Your feelings are valid, Aila. It's important to recognize the progress you've made. You're allowed to protect your peace and prioritize your well-being. Reconnecting with someone from your past doesn't necessarily mean going back to the way things were."

I let out a shaky breath, feeling a bit of the tension release from my shoulders. "But what if he hasn't changed? What if being around him again drags me back into that dark place?"

Dr. Gore gives me a reassuring smile. "You have the power to set boundaries. You don't have to do anything you're not comfortable with. It's also okay to keep your distance if that's what you need to feel safe and stable."

I tilt my head, appreciating his understanding. "I guess I'm just scared. Scared of what reconnecting might bring up, and scared of losing the stability I've fought so hard to achieve."

"Fear is a natural response, especially given what you've been through. It's also a sign that you're aware of your needs and are taking steps to protect yourself. That's a positive thing."

I look down at my hands, feeling a mixture of relief and lingering anxiety. "I just don't know if I'm strong enough to handle this."

"You've shown a lot of strength by recognizing your concerns and seeking help. You're stronger than you realize, Aila. It's important to continue to address these feelings, and we can work through them together." He pauses, then adds, "I recommend we resume regular sessions so we can keep working on this. It will give you a space to express what's been bottled up inside and ensure you have someone in your corner."

"Thank you, Dr. Gore. I think that would help a lot."

"I'm here to support you. We'll take this one step at a time."

The thought of regular sessions gives me a sense of stability, a reminder that I don't have to face everything alone. I have Jaison but he can't understand everything in it's entirety. Though, I know he's no fan of Hunter or Didi, I recall the words of Dr. Gore *"It's okay to keep your distance."*

I walk back to my car, the cool breeze calming my nerves a bit. My mind drifts to the past, to the days with Hunter and Didi. The night that changed everything. It was a crisp autumn evening, the air cool and sharp as it nipped at my skin. Hunter had reached out to me earlier that day, his voice crackling with excitement and mischief. "We've got a plan tonight. You in?" I hesitated, knowing that whatever he had in mind was bound to be trouble. But his charm was always hard to resist.

"What kind of plan?"

He laughed, "Mrs. Gallagher has been a real pain lately. We're gonna break into her house and send a little message from her laptop. Something that'll get her off my back for good." I bit my lip, the idea of breaking into a teacher's house made my stomach twist.

"Hunter, I don't know…"

"Come on. We need your lock-picking skills. You're the best at it, better than me. Didi's in too. It'll be easy, I promise." His words echoed in my mind, the thrill of danger pulling me in despite my better judgment. I agreed, not fully understanding the consequences that would follow. That night, we dressed in dark, inconspicuous clothing, ready to blend into the darkness. Hunter led the way, his confidence never wavering as we approached Mrs. Gallagher's home.

"She'll be out at that fundraising gala," Hunter assured us. "It's the perfect time." I took a deep breath and felt around for the lock-picking tools in my pocket. We reached the house, and I quickly got to work. The familiar click of the lock opening filled me with a strange sense of accomplishment, a skill that had always come naturally to me.

Once inside, we moved quickly. The house was dark and quiet, every creak of the floorboards sending a jolt of adrenaline through me. We found Mrs. Gallagher's laptop on the dining table, just as Hunter had predicted.

"Alright, Aila, do your thing," Hunter whispered, a grin on his face. My teeth clenched as I tensed up. This wasn't the plan. Didi was to hack into the laptop to ultimately send the email while Hunter and I maintained a lookout. I couldn't afford to argue as fear crept up anticipating an early arrival or mishap.

I sat down at the laptop, my fingers flying over the keys as I hacked into her email account. It was easier than I thought, the password was a simple combination of her husband's name and birth year. Within minutes, I was in.

Hunter dictated the message, something vile and incriminating that would surely ruin her reputation. My stomach twisted with each word, but I typed it all out, my hands shaking as I hit send.

The moment I pressed the button, regret washed over me. What had I done? The sound of a car pulling into the driveway snapped me back to reality. "She's back!" I whispered urgently. Panic set in as we scrambled to hide. I darted toward the back of the house, but wasn't quick enough. I found myself crouched behind the living room couch, my heart pounding in my ears. Mrs. Gallagher entered with her husband, their voices muffled but growing closer.

"What are we going to do?" Didi hissed.

"Stay hidden. Wait for them to go upstairs," Hunter replied, his voice surprisingly calm. I stayed as still as possible, my breath shallow. Finally, I heard their footsteps heading towards the stairs. This was my chance. I darted towards the back door, moving as quietly as I could. Just as I reached it, I heard a shout.

"Hey! Who's there?" It was her husband, his voice filled with alarm. I pushed the door open and ran, my legs burning as I sprinted through the large backyard. The sound of footsteps behind me urged me to go faster. I didn't dare look back, my focus set on getting away. My heart hammered in my chest. The fear of being caught drove me forward.

I reached the fence at the end of the yard and climbed over, landing awkwardly on the other side. My ankle twisted painfully, but I forced myself to keep running. The neighborhood was quiet, the streets deserted at this late hour. I ducked into an alleyway, pressing myself against the wall as I tried to catch my breath.

The sound of footsteps faded, and I allowed myself a moment to breathe. My mind raced as the reality of what I'd done sank in. We had sent that email, and Mrs. Gallagher's career would never be the same. I knew then that I could never do something like this again. Hunter and Didi had pulled me into their world of chaos, but I had to get out.

When I finally made it home, I collapsed onto my bed swallowed by my thoughts. The hold they had on me was strong, and it would take years before I fully broke free. Days later, news spread about Mrs. Gallagher's resignation. The email had caused an uproar, and she couldn't convince the school board that she hadn't sent it. The shame and public scrutiny forced her to step down. I watched the fallout from a distance with guilt eating away at me.

I had vowed to never participate in Hunter and Didi's schemes again, but it was a battle I would continue to fight well into my twenties. Now, sitting in my apartment, those memories felt like a lifetime ago. The fear, the thrill, the regret—all of it was still vivid in my mind. I had made mistakes, and I was still paying for them. Hunter's attempt to reconnect had stirred up those old feelings.

The sound of the door opening pulls me from my thoughts. Jaison walks in, a tired smile on his face. "Hey, how was your day?" he asks, dropping his bag by the door.

I force a smile, "It was okay. Just… thinking about some things." He walks over and plants a kiss on my forehead.

"Well, I'm here now. Let's make tonight better." As we settle into our evening routine, I remind myself that I am no longer that scared teenager. I have grown, learned, and found a way to move forward. The past will always be a part of me, but it doesn't have to define my future. I'm stronger now and ready to face whatever challenges come my way.

CHAPTER 26
CARTER

I park a few blocks away from Booker's house, just as I have every other night this week. The cold wind brushes against my face as I walk the familiar route to her neighborhood, taking care to stay in the shadows. I slip into the side yard, crouching behind the shrubs that line the property. From this vantage point, I can see the driveway and the garage door. The street is quiet, almost too quiet, but it's the perfect cover.

My breath comes out in controlled, even puffs. I know Booker's routine well enough by now. She'll arrive home around this time, pulling into the garage and losing herself in her phone as she settles in. It's her pattern, her predictable habit that I am going to exploit. Right on schedule, I see her car approaching. It pulls into the driveway, the headlights cutting through the growing darkness. I press myself lower, ensuring the bushes conceal me from view. She pulls into the garage, and as the door begins to lower, I move swiftly. Timing is everything.

I slip under the garage door just before it shuts, moving with the stealth and precision I have honed over years on the force. The darkness of the garage envelops me, and I hear the car door open and then close with a muffled thud. She is engrossed in her phone, her face illuminated by its faint glow. She doesn't even notice me.

I approach her silently, my gloved hands ready. The garage is filled with the scent of oil and metal, the oppressive silence pressing down on us. I am inches away from her now. She is still distracted, swiping through whatever work has followed her home. In a swift, calculated move, I wrap my arm around her neck, my other hand clamping over her mouth to suppress any screams. She struggles, her phone clattering to the concrete floor, the screen shattering on impact. She tries to scream, but the sound is muffled. I tighten my grip, feeling her body thrash against mine as she tries to break free.

Her nails claw at my shirt, struggling to catch a grip. I hold firm. Her strength wanes quickly, the lack of oxygen taking its toll. I feel a cold, detached fury as I hold on, determined. Her body sags against me, as her struggle weakens, until finally, she goes crashing down with a loud thud. I grip my hands around her throat firmly and squeeze. Her life drains away and I wait until I am certain she is gone.

I check for a pulse, feeling nothing. Booker is dead. I take a moment to calm my racing heart, the adrenaline still coursing through me. This was necessary, I tell myself. She was a threat to everything, and now that threat is gone.

I straighten up, surveying the scene. The garage is dimly lit by a single overhead bulb. I move methodically, making sure there is no trace of my presence. I crouch down and observe her phone. The screen and glass back have shattered as a result of the fall. I can't decipher what she had been doing on it prior. I take a final look around, ensuring everything is in order.

My footsteps are silent on the cold concrete as I make my way through the garage and into the house using her key. The faint scent of mint lingers in the kitchen. I pause, listening for any sign of life, but there is nothing. The house is as silent as a tomb. I move quickly, making my way to her study. The door is slightly ajar, and I push it open, slipping inside.

The room is small, cluttered with papers and files. A large desk sits against the far wall, a laptop closed on its surface. I move to the desk and rummage through the papers. Booker has been meticulous, her notes organized and detailed. I find a folder labeled "Carter & Phoebe," and my heart skips a beat. I open the folder and begin to read. Booker has been building a case against us for a while. She has statements from witnesses, descriptions, and even photos of Phoebe engaging in daily activities. It is clear she has been following Phoebe, hoping to catch her in something incriminating. My anger flares as I realize the extent of her surveillance.

I flip through the photos, my breath catching when I see one of Phoebe entering a community center. Booker must have found it significant enough to include. I gather all the files and make my way to the backdoor. I slip out, closing and locking the door behind me.

Booker has been thorough, but she has underestimated me. After canvassing quite a distance on foot, I find a secluded spot near an abandoned lot, the perfect place to dispose of the evidence. I pull the files from the bag, one by one, and set them on the ground. The flames from my lighter flicker as I set the papers alight, watching as they curl and blacken in the fire. The heat from the flames warms my hands as I listen to the faint crackling of the burning paper.

The lengthy walk back to my parked car allows

ample time to reflect. Booker had been a threat, and I had neutralized that threat. It was as simple as that. I had done what needed to be done to protect myself and Phoebe. The darkness of the night had covered my actions, and I would ensure that no light ever shone on them.

As I sit at my kitchen table, I can't help but become lost in my thoughts. Booker's investigation into Phoebe and me threatens more than just our present; it has the potential to uncover my past, a past I've worked so hard to leave behind and conceal. My history starts at the precinct, and that's where I want it to stay. I'm not only protecting Phoebe; I'm protecting my legacy. Though I appreciate the lessons and skills my past has taught me about protecting my family, there's too much at stake to let it resurface.

I reflect on a time when my mother saved me. I see her face clearly in my mind, worn and determined. She always said I was meant for something better, something greater than the tragedy I was born into. My father, a man who had succumbed to the darker side of life, left us with nothing but scars and a burning need to escape. My mother made sure I had that chance.

I remember the day she sat me down and told me I was going away to college. I had just turned eighteen, and the idea of leaving felt both exhilarating and terrifying. "You're going to study criminology," she said, her voice firm but gentle. "You have a gift, and it's time you use it to build a better life for yourself."

She sent me off to college in another state to study criminology, my passion. My life was full of possibility, and for a while, it seemed like I had escaped. I immersed myself in my studies, eager to carve out a new path. But life has a way of shattering even the best-laid plans. Just as I was starting to find my footing, I put trust in the wrong individual, uprooting everything, and forcing me to start fresh once again, this time in Rutledge.

Rutledge was a chance for a new beginning, a place where I could bury the past and build something solid. I joined the police force, working my way up to detective. The work was challenging but fulfilling, and for the first time in a long time, I felt like I was making a difference. I built a solid legacy as a successful detective, and I can't let it be shattered by someone I taught and trained. Booker was my protégé, someone I had taken under my wing, and she quickly became the very force that threatened to unravel everything.

I glance at Phoebe, her eyes closed as she rests on the couch. She's been through so much, and I can't let her suffer. I walk over to her and brush a strand of hair from her face. She stirs, opening her eyes and looking up at me with concern. "Honey, are you okay?" she asks, her voice soft.

"I'm fine," I say, forcing a smile. "Just thinking."

"About what?"

"About us. About the future. We're going to be okay, Phoebe. I promise. Come to bed." I lean in to assist her up and into our bedroom. We slip into our night clothes and into bed, cuddling through the night.

CHAPTER 27
AILA

I stand at the edge of the park, feeling a heavy weight in my chest as I watch the crowd gather for Gary Robinson's public funeral. The setting sun casts a golden hue over the area, giving everything an almost ethereal quality. Rows of white folding chairs are set up on the grassy lawn, facing a makeshift stage adorned with flowers and candles. People move quietly, finding their seats, their expressions somber and reflective.

Gary Robinson was the Shadow Stalker's fifth victim. I feel a deep sadness at his loss, mingled with a sense of failure. Though Gary wasn't known as a good person, no one deserves to die the way he did. I believe there are other ways to deal with people who make poor choices, ways that don't involve ending their lives.

I walk slowly toward the gathering, each step feeling heavier than the last. The quiet murmur of conversations fills the air, punctuated by the occasional sob. I find a place to stand near the back, close enough to hear but far enough to observe without being noticed. My eyes scan the crowd, taking in the mix of faces, each one reflecting different shades of grief.

The ceremony begins with a soft hymn, sung by a woman from the local church. Her voice is chilling, carrying over the heads of the assembled mourners. As the song ends, a man steps up to the microphone. He is from the church Gary had attended a few times, though sporadically. His face is lined with sorrow as he begins to speak.

"Gary Robinson was a great soul," he starts, his voice trembling slightly. "He made mistakes, as we all do, but he was seeking redemption. He came to our church, searching for something greater than himself, searching for peace."

I listen intently, my heart aching. The man's words paint a picture of Gary that I hadn't known. I feel a pang of guilt for judging him based on the stories I'd heard. As the eulogy continues, the speaker's words grow more poignant, describing Gary's struggles and his attempts to find a better path. The crowd around me begins to tear up, their grief intense in the evening air.

"And now," the man says, his voice breaking, "we must find it in our hearts to forgive. Forgive Gary for his sins, forgive the one who took him from us, and pray for an end to this senseless violence."

Tears well up in my eyes as I glance around at the mourners. They are all deeply moved, many of them openly weeping. But then my gaze catches on something unusual. A woman, standing a little apart from the crowd, catches my eye. She wears a white flowing dress adorned with printed flowers, vibrant and colorful, completely out of place at such a somber event.

The woman is young and blonde, her hair cascading in soft waves around her shoulders. What strikes me most is her expression. While everyone else is lost in their sorrow, she seems almost content, happy even. She stands there alone, observing the ceremony from a distance, her eyes bright and alert.

I can't shake the feeling that something is off about her. Why would she wear such a bright, cheerful dress to a vigil? And why does she seem so unaffected by the grief around her? I watch her carefully, planning to approach her when the ceremony ends. I need to understand why she is here and why she seems so out of place.

The eulogy comes to a close with a prayer, and I take a deep breath, readying myself to move toward the woman. But as the crowd begins to disperse, I realize she is gone. I scan the area frantically, searching for any sign of her, but she has slipped away before I can reach her. I stand there as frustration mounts.

As the crowd continues to thin out, I decide to stay a bit longer, hoping she might reappear. I wander around the park. The sun has set by now, and the dim light from the streetlamps cast long shadows across the grass. I approach a small group of people who are still lingering near the stage, hoping to overhear something useful."

"Can you imagine? Not a single person from his family showed up," one woman says to her friend, shaking her head sadly.

"I heard they were estranged," the friend replies. "Maybe they couldn't face it."

Why would Gary's family choose not to attend his vigil? What had happened to create such a rift? My thoughts are interrupted by the sight of a man I recognize from the police station. He is an officer, standing near the back of the gathering, looking around with a concerned expression.

I make my way over to him, hoping he might have some answers. "Officer Jenkins," I call out, catching his attention. He turns to me, his expression softening slightly.

"Hey, good to see you. Tough night, huh?"

"Yeah," I reply, nodding. "Do you know anything about Gary's family? Why they didn't come?"

Jenkins sighs, rubbing the back of his neck. "It's a sad story, really. Gary had a lot of issues, and he pushed his family away over the years. They couldn't handle his behavior anymore, and they cut ties with him a while back. I guess they didn't feel like they could face this."

I nod, digesting the information. "I understand. It's just… there was a woman here, dressed in a white floral dress. She didn't seem to be mourning like the others. Do you know who she is?"

Jenkins frowns, shaking his head. "I didn't notice anyone like that. But if she stood out to you, maybe she's worth looking into. You've got good instincts."

"Thanks. I wish I had more. Take care of yourself."

The crowd has mostly dispersed, leaving only a few stragglers behind. I finally decide to head home, my mind still clouded with suspicions. The walk back to my apartment is quiet, the streets almost deserted. When I get home, I find myself unable to rest. I sit at my desk, pulling out a notebook and jotting down everything I can remember about the woman. Her dress, her demeanor, the way she had observed the ceremony from a distance. I need to keep these details fresh in my mind, in case I encounter her again.

I log into Echo to check the Shadow Stalker updates page. I notice a flurry of notifications. Many users have tagged me in a public post, and others have forwarded it directly to me. My curiosity piqued, I click on the most recent tag and my screen fills with a post written by a woman.

Today, I attended my abuser's vigil. In contrast to the overwhelming sadness around me, I felt relieved and renewed. Imagining seeing him moments before his execution, if he had ever been made to pay for his crimes through the justice system, seemed like a far-fetched dream. Sexual offenders only receive a slap on the wrist for their crimes, as if they're considered petty crimes.

Her words are bold and unapologetic. They send a chill through me as I continue to read.

Because I couldn't be one of the observers in a death row execution, I found solace in watching him being buried in the ground. If this is how he had to pay for his crimes, so be it. The Shadow Stalker has done what the justice system failed to do. She's saved many people and protected many women from a monster. For that, I thank her. If you were a victim, suffer no longer. Peace be unto you.

My heart sinks into my stomach as I enlarge the profile photo attached to the post. The image is of a young blonde woman, her face serene and almost joyful. It's the woman from the vigil—the one in the white floral dress. So, Gary Robinson was a predator. The realization crashes over me, leaving me stunned and mind-blown. All the sadness and pity I felt for him earlier now mixed with a sense of revulsion and confusion. The woman at the vigil wasn't just any mourner; she was one of his victims.

I lean back in my chair, the room around me blurring as I process this new information. The implications are staggering. Gary Robinson wasn't just a troubled soul; he was a monster hiding in plain sight. And the woman had every reason to feel the way she did. On one hand, I understand her relief and sense of justice. On the other, I'm deeply troubled by the idea of vigilante justice and the dangerous precedent it sets. The Shadow Stalker, praised and thanked by this woman, may have taken the law into their own hands, bypassing the justice system entirely.

I scroll through the comments on the post, seeing a mix of reactions. Some people echo her sentiments, praising the Shadow Stalker for their actions. Others are horrified, condemning the vigilante and expressing concern over the destruction of legal justice. I can't help but think about the other victims of the Shadow Stalker's attacks. Were they all like Gary Robinson?

I close my eyes, trying to steady my mind. I need to approach this carefully. It's a crucial piece of the puzzle, but it also complicates things. If the Shadow Stalker is targeting predators, it suggests a pattern, a motive rooted in a sense of protection and retribution. But that doesn't make it right.

CHAPTER 28
CARTER

The early morning light filters through the blinds of my office window. It's just after 5:00 AM, and the precinct is still and silent. Booker's desk is on the opposite side of the work floor. I know I have about an hour before the first officers start trickling in. I stand up, smoothing out my shirt and adjusting my tie, making sure I look as composed as possible. Every step echoes in the empty precinct as I walk over to her workspace.

Her desk is neat, meticulously organized, just like her investigations. I start with the drawers, pulling them open one by one, carefully rifling through the contents. Pens, sticky notes, case files, nothing out of the ordinary so far. But then, in the bottom drawer, tucked away beneath some files, I find what I'm looking for – another folder labeled with my name and Phoebe's.

I open the folder, my heart pounding in my chest. Inside, there are more documents, more evidence that Booker has been compiling against Phoebe, and now, against me. Statements from witnesses, photographs, timelines. She's been thorough, methodical, and dangerously close to uncovering everything.

I scan the documents quickly. What if she has more evidence stored digitally? I glance over at her computer, the screen dark and lifeless. But if Booker was smart enough to conduct this investigation off the books, she likely hasn't left any digital trail that could be easily found. She wouldn't risk it, especially if it meant accusing the station's lead detective of a serious crime.

Destroying the files is my only option. I grab the folder and head back to my office, careful to keep my movements calm and collected. I lock the door behind me and go to the small shredder in the corner of the room. One by one, I feed the documents through the machine, watching as the evidence of Booker's investigation is reduced to tiny strips of paper.

By the time the folder is empty, I'm sweating. I wipe my forehead and take a deep breath, trying to steady my nerves. There can't be any trace left. I gather the shredded paper and dump it into the waste bin, covering it with other trash to make it less conspicuous.

As I return to my desk, I see the first few officers arriving. The quiet murmur of their voices and the sounds of footsteps fill the precinct, slowly bringing it to life. I sit down and try to focus on my work. Midway through the morning, I notice the growing confusion among my colleagues. Booker hasn't shown up for work, and people are starting to talk. Harper and Jenkins stop by my office, their expressions concerned.

"Have you heard from Booker?" Harper asks, leaning against the doorframe. "She's usually here by now."

I shake my head, feigning concern. "No, I haven't. It's not like her to be late."

Jenkins nods, "We tried calling her cell a few times,

but there's no answer. Maybe it's some sort of emergency."

"Could be," I say, keeping my voice steady. "But it's strange that she wouldn't let anyone know."

By noon, the concern has turned into worry. The precinct buzzes with whispers and speculation. Booker's absence is unusual, and everyone is starting to feel uneasy. Patrol is dispatched to conduct a wellness check at her home. I spend a lot of time in my office, pretending to be buried in paperwork, but outside of my office doors, my ears are tuned to every conversation around me.

The minutes tick by slowly. I can't help but consider what they'll find when they get to Booker's house. My stomach twists with anxiety. I head to the break room to fetch a cup of coffee, hoping it will be refreshening. Harper and Jenkins joins me.

"Captain sent a patrol to her place," Harper says. "They should be there soon."

"I hope she's okay," I say.

Jenkins shrugs. "Yes. It's odd but I'm sure we're all just shaken up and on edge." I nod, keeping my face neutral. Inside, my mind is racing and I'm struggling to suppress my nervousness.

The precinct is a hive of activity as the search for Booker continues. Captain Walsh approaches my office with sternness etched in his expression. He knocks on the doorframe before stepping inside. "Carter, can I have a word?"

I look up, forcing a neutral expression. "Of course, Captain. What's up?"

Walsh sighs, rubbing the back of his neck. "I hate to ask this of you, especially with everything going on, but we need someone to handle today's tasks on the Shadow Stalker case. We haven't heard from Booker, and you know the case best."

I reluctantly agree, "I understand, Captain. I'll handle it."

"Thank you," he says, sounding genuinely grateful. "We're still awaiting permission to enter Booker's home. There's been no response to knocks and calls, but everything looks fine. Her car isn't in the driveway, so she may not even be home. But we need to make sure."

"Hopefully, we'll get some answers about Booker soon."

Walsh gives me a sympathetic look. "I appreciate it, Carter. Just for today, until we can get a hold of her."

As he leaves, I let out a deep breath I hadn't realized I was holding. I was angry when Booker was allowed to take over my case, but now I have the chance to see exactly what she's been up to. I log into the system and access her files on the Shadow Stalker case, eager to see if she's made any real progress outside of her pursuit of Phoebe and me.

I scan through her notes, my eyes narrowing as I read. Booker previously developed a theory that the killer is a woman targeting sex offenders. It's an angle she wanted to announce to the public but was advised against to avoid creating an uproar of support for the vigilante. The department agreed that such a revelation could slow the case, as tips and community help might dwindle if people thought the killer was doing a good deed.

I continue reading, my frustration growing. Booker's next plan was to inform the known sex offenders in the area, but she hadn't even thought to trace the victims as I had. Rookie mistake. The victims hold the key. They always do. Yet, I can't lead the team in this direction without raising suspicion, so I need to come up with a plan to keep everyone busy.

I step out of my office and gather the team to assign them tasks, deliberately repeating previous efforts and reinterviewing past witnesses. It's busy work, meant to keep them occupied while I focus on the real leads.

"Harper, I need you to go through the witness statements again. See if there's anything we missed," I say.

"Will do, Carter."

"Jenkins, I want you to reinterview the managers of Gary Robinson. See if anyone remembers something new."

"Got it."

As they disperse, I retreat back to my office. I dive back into Booker's files. I can see the flaws in her approach. She focused too much on the profile of the killer and not enough on the victims. It's a common mistake, but a dangerous one. Each victim has a story, a connection that will help me stop the Shadow Stalker.

CHAPTER 29
AILA

Discovering Gary was an offender leaves me feeling conflicted. She may not know it, but the lady in the floral dress is onto something. She's convinced the Shadow Stalker unknowingly delivered an outlawed form of justice in murdering Gary Robinson. I'm convinced it was her intent. I spend my day locked on my laptop uncovering the pasts of each victim in detail hoping for connections.

I start with Liam Harris, recalling his ex-wife had given a strange warning about his behavior, and I can't shake the feeling that she knew more than she let on. I delve into his background, my fingers flying over the keyboard as I search through public records and old news articles.

Liam Harris was a registered sex offender. The details of his crimes are sickening—he was found to have inappropriate photos of children in his possession. He claimed the briefcase they were found in belonged to a coworker, but his ex-wife didn't believe him. She threatened to report him but never did. Instead, she filed for divorce and full custody of their children. Liam didn't contest it. Later, he was convicted of crimes against minors and served a prison sentence before being released to Rutledge City, where he registered as a high-risk offender.

I slump over, staring at the screen. The pieces are starting to fit together, but I need more information. I pull up the files on the other victims—Jacob Garcia, Daniel Edwards, and Hank Easton. Each one of them was a registered sex offender. Their crimes varied, but the pattern was clear. They all had histories of abusing others.

How did I miss this? It was right in front of me the whole time. I slam my fist on the desk, unable to contain my frustration. I need to get this out to the public. I open Echo, to share updates on the Shadow Stalker case. My followers have been demanding new information. My fingers move swiftly over the keys as I start my post.

Update on critical developments in the Shadow Stalker case. After delving deeper into the backgrounds of the five men who were murdered, I have uncovered a disturbing pattern. Liam Harris, Jacob Garcia, Daniel Edwards, Hank Easton, and Gary Robinson were all registered sex offenders. Their crimes are public records. This revelation has brought a chilling new perspective to the case.

While it is now confirmed that all five victims were sex offenders, it is important to remember that the killer's motives are still alleged. We cannot condone vigilantism, regardless of the victims' past actions. Justice must be served through the proper channels, not through murder.

I understand the frustration and anger that such crimes can evoke, but we must let the law take its course. The

idea of a vigilante taking justice into their own hands is dangerous and sets a troubling precedent. It is our duty to find this killer and ensure that they face the consequences of their actions in a court of law.

Please stay vigilant and report any suspicious activity to the authorities. Your cooperation is crucial in bringing the Shadow Stalker to justice. Thank you for your continued support and understanding.

I hit 'post,' watching as the message goes live. Within seconds, notifications start flooding in—likes, shares, comments. The response is immediate and intense. I scroll through the comments, seeing a mix of outrage, support, and fear. People are scared, and rightfully so. The idea of a vigilante targeting sex offenders is both terrifying and, for some, oddly comforting. It's a complex, emotionally charged issue, and I can see the debate unfolding in real-time.

I close my laptop and lean back in my chair, rubbing my temples. There's a woman out there, taking justice into her own hands. Innocent people could get caught in the crossfire. I need to figure out who she is and stop her before she strikes again.

My trip to the mall proves to be a pain. The mall is overcrowded with shoppers, loiterers, and people who take to the building to escape their day. It's a bright, casual space with high ceilings and a skylight that lets in natural light. The air is filled with the scents of perfume and different foods from the center court. I head straight to my preferred clothing store on the second floor, hoping to find a new pair of jeans. I've been stress-eating since I started working on the Shadow Stalker case, and my pants have started to feel uncomfortably tight.

I'm welcomed by the sight of neatly organized racks of clothing, sorted by color. The walls are lined with bright yellows, soft pastels, deep blues, and striking blacks. The associates are scattered around, some helping customers while others wait by the counter. The atmosphere is calm.

I make my way to the denim section, feeling the different fabrics between my fingers as I search for the perfect pair of jeans. It's a soothing routine sifting through the options. I hear a familiar voice, drawing my attention.

"Aila! It's been a while." Didi's voice calls in a cheerful tone. I force a smile.

"Hi, Didi. Yeah, it has. How have you been?"

"Great! Well, not really. Hunter's been trying to get a hold of you. He's been worried." My stomach twists at the mention of Hunter.

"My contact information changed. That's probably why he hasn't been able to reach me."

Didi sighs dramatically. "He misses you, Aila. Why don't you give me your new details, and I'll pass them along to him?"

I hesitate, not eager to see Hunter or even Didi again. Our past is complicated, and I've been avoiding it for a reason. "I'm not sure, Didi. I've got a lot on my plate right now."

Didi's tone softens, almost pleading. "Seriously? He's family."

I close my eyes for a moment, feeling the weight of Didi's words. Family. The concept feels foreign to me lately. "Alright," I finally say.

"Great! You two need to reconnect."

"Thanks, Didi."

She shifts the conversation to what brings me into

the mall and I explain that I'm simply looking for new pants. Her eyes dart to my hips immediately.

"You're certainly filling out. Not quite the Aila that I was used to," she says with a playful snicker. Though I don't find the comment funny. Didi always had a way of masking her insults with jokes that it seemed only I was ever able to pick up on. Possibly because she only seemed to ever target me.

As I slip my phone back into my pocket, I brace myself for the inevitable communication, hoping it won't come at the worst possible time. I pull out a pair of jeans and head to the fitting rooms at the back of the store. The mirrors reflect my image back at me, and I can't help but scrutinize my appearance. My face looks tired, with dark circles under my eyes. My body feels heavier, the result of too many late-night snacks and stress-induced cravings. I slip on the jeans, appreciating the way they fit snugly around my waist but still give me room to breathe.

I step out of the fitting room to check myself in the larger mirrors outside. The jeans look good, and I decide to buy them. As I head back to the rack to grab a couple more pairs in different colors, I let my mind wander back to Didi's words. Will it be like old times, or will the distance and time apart have changed everything?

The cashier smiles at me as I approach the counter, a young woman with a friendly demeanor. "Did you find everything you were looking for?"

"Yes, thanks."

She scans my items and bags them quickly. "We have a sale on tops if you're interested," she says, gesturing to a nearby display.

I shake my head. "Not today, but thanks." I find a quiet bench near a large indoor fountain and sit down, watching the water cascade over the smooth stones. The sound is soothing, a small break from the turmoil in my mind. Finally, with my bags full, I head back to my car to make my way home.

CHAPTER 30
CARTER

The precinct feels like a tomb today. The usually lively hallways are eerily silent. News of Detective Booker's murder has hit us all hard. I sit at my desk, staring blankly at the scattered documents in front of me. Booker was found in her garage, strangled. It's a brutal end for someone who dedicated her life to seeking justice.

Captain Walsh has called a meeting. We gather in the conference room, the atmosphere heavy with shock. The room is packed, yet it feels empty. Everyone is here, but the lively chatter and camaraderie that usually fill the space are conspicuously absent.

Walsh stands at the front with a somber look. He clears his throat, and the room shifts focus to him. "We've lost one of our own," he begins, his voice steady but filled with emotion. "Detective Booker was more than a colleague; she was a friend, a mentor, a dedicated member of our team. Her loss is a tragedy, and we will honor her memory by continuing the work she started." I feel a lump form in my throat. Booker was relentless, always pushing to solve the case, to bring justice to the victims. Walsh continues, "We believe Booker's death is related to the

Shadow Stalker case. While the evidence is not conclusive, the community believes she was targeted for getting too close to the truth. We must proceed with caution and determination."

He pauses, looking around the room, his eyes lingering on each of us. "Detective Carter will resume control over the Shadow Stalker case. I know this is a heavy burden, but Carter, you have our full support." I nod, acknowledging the weight of the responsibility. I stand up, taking a deep breath.

"Thank you, Captain. Booker was dedicated to this case, and I will honor her by seeing it through to the end. We will find the person responsible for these heinous crimes." The room is silent, everyone absorbing the gravity of the situation. Walsh dismisses the meeting, and we all file out slowly, each of us lost in our thoughts.

I head back to my desk, but I can't sit still. The need to act, to do something, anything, propels me to Booker's cubicle. It appears untouched. Her desk is neat, everything in its place. I feel a pang of sadness as I look at the framed photo of her kids on the corner of her desk. I start going through her files, pretending to look for clues. I feel a deep respect for her as I read through her work. She was thorough, always thinking a step ahead. But that very dedication is what landed her where she is.

We move to her house, a team of investigators combing through every inch. The exterior is unremarkable, a typical suburban home. The garage, where she was found, is a mess of tools and gardening supplies. Nothing seems out of place, no signs of a struggle beyond the obvious.

Inside, her home is tidy, almost sterile. Photos of her children are everywhere, a testament to the love she had for them. I can't imagine what they're going through right now. We interview her ex-husband and her kids. The ex seems genuinely distraught, with no animosity, no hint of anything that would make the department suspect him. Her kids are devastated. Their grief is raw and painful to witness.

Back at the precinct, we interview the staff, trying to piece together Booker's last day. Everyone has the same story: they saw her at the end of the day, she seemed fine, nothing out of the ordinary. I give my own statement, recounting our last conversation, but I tell a different story. We had a brief conversation about typical case updates. Though I was no longer on the case, she ran her thoughts by me, valuing my general input.

We search her desk again, combing through every drawer, every file. Still nothing. It's another clean, calculated attack. No room for error and no clues left behind. Booker didn't fit the MO of the Shadow Stalker's previous victims. She wasn't a sex offender; she was a cop. This could eventually raise questions. But the fact that she got too close to something or stumbled onto a truth that put her in the killer's crosshairs is motive enough.

Just then, Jenkins makes an announcement. The Shadow Stalker Updates page has just released a bombshell. The announcement is causing an uproar, both inside the precinct and in the community. They've announced that the serial killer is targeting sexual offenders, a detail we had intentionally kept under wraps. Irritation brews as I follow along reading the post. The post reads:

As stated before, It is alleged, but not confirmed, that the Shadow Stalker is targeting sexual offenders. The recent murder of Detective Booker highlights the lengths this individual is willing to go to protect their

mission. This is no vigilante; this is a person with a twisted sense of justice who must be stopped.

The comments are a mixed bag, reflecting the division within the community. Some people express their fear, saying they don't mind staying out of the Shadow Stalker's way and criticizing the police department's effectiveness. Others passionately agree that the Shadow Stalker must be stopped, calling the actions of the killer evil and misguided. The fact that people believe Booker's murder to be the work of the Shadow Stalker gives me a strange sense of relief. At least it means they won't immediately suspect foul play from within the department. But I know it's only a matter of time before the city demands answers, before they demand a culprit to be brought to justice.

Just as I'm trying to process all of this, an officer rushes over to my desk. "Carter, we've found something at Booker's house," he says, his voice urgent. "Hair fibers. They were found near the bedroom and in the kitchen. The strands don't match Booker's hair color, so we believe they belong to another party."

My heart skips. "Hair fibers?" I repeat, my mind racing back to the scene. Had I gone near the bedroom? I remember being in the kitchen, but I was careful, wasn't I? My hair is short, but my beard... Could I have left a strand or two behind? I start to panic, recalling every step I took in Booker's house. I try to keep my composure, nodding at the officer. "Get those fibers to the lab immediately. We need results as soon as possible."

The officer hurries off, leaving me alone with my thoughts. I feel a cold sweat break out on my forehead. I was careful, but accidents happen. I know I wore gloves, but did I do enough? I can't afford to make mistakes, not now, not with everything on the line. I sit back in my chair, staring at the computer screen but not really seeing it. If those hair fibers match mine, I'll have a lot of explaining to do. The department already has its hands full and the last thing we need is suspicion turning inward.

I try to focus on the facts. The hair fibers don't match Booker's, which means they belong to someone else who was in her house. If it's not mine, then it could be pinned on another party. But if it is mine... I can't think about that right now. I have to stay focused. The next few days will be agonizing as we wait for the results of the hair strands.

As the precinct empties, I gather my things and head towards the exit. The moment I step out, I'm met with a wall of reporters and media personnel, their cameras flashing, their microphones thrust toward me.

"Detective Carter, do you feel any guilt for Detective Booker's murder since it's taken so long to find the killer?" one reporter shouts.

"Why did the department withhold important details about the victims' criminal backgrounds?" another one asks, in a voice tinged with accusation.

"How does it feel to be back in charge of the case, and what are your plans to move it to closure?" a third voice calls out.

I raise a hand to shield my eyes from the bright lights and take a deep breath. "I apologize on behalf of the department for concealing certain information," I say, my voice steady. "However, we back our stance on not releasing those details sooner. Our goal was to prevent exactly what we're seeing now—a community in uproar, with many supporting the actions of a killer. This doesn't help the case, and it encourages the Shadow Stalker to strike again."

I pause, letting my words sink in. "My first course of action is to get the Shadow Stalker page taken down. It's interfering with the case and putting more lives at risk." The reporters continue to shout questions, but I lower my head and push through the crowd, making my way to my vehicle. The cacophony of voices fades slightly as I break free from the throng of reporters, but their questions linger.

I climb into my car, closing the door behind me, and let out a long breath. The silence inside the vehicle is a welcome relief. I rest my head against the steering wheel, trying to gather my thoughts. The other officers don't give statements, following my lead and shielding themselves as they hurry to their own cars.

I start the engine and pull out of the parking lot. The image of Booker's lifeless body in her garage flashes in my mind and I swiftly push it to the back. If I'm going to clean the mess made while working alongside the department trying to unravel the truth, I have to have a clear mind. Booker didn't deserve to be crucified, but neither do I. When push comes to shove, shove.

CHAPTER 31
AILA

Temperatures have begun to drop signaling the winter is near. I find myself nuzzled on my loveseat, with my laptop resting on my lap. The glow from the small screen illuminates the dark room. Jaison is home early, but catching up on much-needed sleep. A steaming mug of raspberry tea sits beside me, untouched, as I scroll through the notifications on the Shadow Stalker updates page. My eyes widen when I see a name that stands out among the sea of usernames: Blake Foster. My heart skips a beat. *The* Blake Foster, has engaged with my page.

I recall seeing him days ago in the sports lounge before quickly running out. Blake is a local celebrity in Rutledge. He owns Foster's Nightclub and several successful restaurants downtown. His venues are the heartbeat of the city's nightlife, drawing in celebrities and tourists alike. For him to interact with the Shadow Stalker updates page is monumental. His influence could bring an unprecedented level of attention and support. Curiosity and a sense of urgency propel me to click on the notification. Blake has left a comment on one of the posts. I lean in closer to read it, my pulse quickening.

While I despise predators, I don't believe the Shadow Stalker is justified in their mission to illegally take them down. However, I support the motive of the page and what the operator has done to bring light to the news of the prowling killer.

My breath catches in my throat. Blake Foster is supporting the page's efforts. This is huge. I quickly navigate to his profile to see the shared posts. His feed is filled with likes and shares from the Shadow Stalker updates page. My heart races as I read through the comments on his posts. Some people echo his sentiments, agreeing that while they hate predators, vigilantism isn't the answer. Others are less supportive, aligning with the police department's stance that the page is causing more harm than good. One comment catches my eye and makes my blood boil.

Isn't it possible that the owner of this page is the killer? Seems suspicious to me.

I clench my fists, my nails digging into my palms. How can they be so ungrateful? I've put myself at risk to bring this information to the public. I've been nothing but transparent about the dangers lurking in Rutledge. The insinuation that I could be the killer is infuriating.

I take a deep breath, trying to calm myself. I type a response, my fingers flying over the keys.

Thank you for your comment. I understand your concerns, but I assure you, my only goal is to keep the community informed and safe. The Shadow Stalker

updates page is about shedding light on a dangerous situation and providing vital information to the public. We all want the same thing: to see justice served.

I glance back at Blake's profile and see that he's defending the page against some of the harsher critics.

I believe the operator of the Shadow Stalker updates page is doing a service to the community by providing information that the police have withheld. It's important to stay informed, especially when lives are at stake. Accusing the page owner of being the killer is baseless and unhelpful.

I feel a wave of gratitude. His support is not only validating but also crucial in shifting public opinion. With his backing, more people might start to see the value in the information I'm sharing. I close my laptop and take a deep breath, letting the tension slowly seep from my body. I stand and stretch, feeling the strain in my shoulders and neck. The past few days have been relentless, and I realize I've barely slept properly.

I can't help but think about the implications of Blake's support. His influence could be a double-edged sword. While it brings more attention and legitimacy to the page, it also means increased scrutiny.

I decide to join Jaison in bed. His warmth is exactly what I need right now for relief. I lie down next to him, resting my head on his chest. He stirs slightly, his body adjusting to accommodate me, and then his arm wraps around me in a familiar, comforting embrace. I feel his heartbeat against my cheek, a steady, calming rhythm.

On his nightstand, his phone buzzes, the screen illuminating with a notification. I glance over and see a text message light up the screen.

You can count on me.
I'll take care of it. We'll talk more tomorrow.

The name saved indicates it's from a woman. For a moment, I feel a flicker of curiosity and temptation to pick up his phone and read more, but I resist. I trust Jaison. We've been together for eight years, and in all that time, he's never given me a reason to doubt him. Even though the after-hours text is a bit unusual, I'm confident it's harmless.

As I lie there, I let my mind wander back to the early days of our relationship. Jaison has been devoted to me from the very beginning. He used to tell me that he fell for me the moment he saw me. I smile at the memory, feeling grateful that I haven't had to deal with scandals or betrayals. Jaison is loving and trustworthy. At 35, he still has the same youthful appearance that he had when we met. His looks often turn heads when we're out in public. My mom always jokes that I've met my match in terms of physical attractiveness, saying that Jaison and I make a flawless couple.

But it wasn't just his looks that hooked me. It was his charm, his ability to make me feel like the most important person in his world. I didn't have that kind of affection growing up, and finding it in Jaison felt like finding a missing piece of myself. He has a way of making me feel seen and valued, something I deeply cherish.

I snuggle closer to him, feeling his warmth seep into me. His presence is soothing, and the tension from the day slowly fades away. I let myself be consumed by the comfort of his embrace, my eyelids growing heavy. As I slip into sleep, my mind quiets. In this moment, I feel safe and loved, wrapped in the arms of the man who has always been there for me.

CHAPTER 32
CARTER

To start my morning, I put in the request for a subpoena on the Shadow Stalker Updates page and demand a rush, hoping to get some traction before things spiral even further out of control. Once I finish, I head out for a break, but it's hardly a break. I've decided to visit the community center where Channing holds his support group meetings. It's a long shot, but I need answers. The cold air bites at my skin as I step outside, moving swiftly to my car.

I arrive at the community center and it's buzzing with activity, different from before. Members loitering in the hallways engrossed in conversations, people hurrying to meetings, the typical hustle and bustle of a weekday morning. I embrace the warmth of the building after stepping inside from the declining temperatures. I spot Channing in a small office, busy with paperwork. He sees me and gestures for me to wait outside in the hall. Eventually, he steps out, holding a cigarette. I brace myself for the request I know is coming. He gestures for me to step outside with him. His breath is visible in the cold, curling into the air as he lights the cigarette and takes a drag.

Rubbing my hands together while simultaneously

blowing into them, I decide to jump right in. "Channing, I need to ask you about the dark-haired girl who spoke passionately at the last meeting," I say.

He looks taken aback, his eyes narrowing. "For privacy purposes, I can't release any details about who attends these meetings," he replies, clearly confused and a bit offended by my directness.

I flash my badge, hoping it will lend some weight to my request. "I'm a detective, Channing. This is important."

His expression hardens. "I understand the law, Detective. If you want that kind of confidential information, you'll need a warrant. Without it, I can't help you."

I get a rush of frustration but try to keep it under control. "I'm just trying to stop the Shadow Stalker. I need to know why she was there, if she's… a victim." The last word feels heavy on my tongue, the implication making my stomach churn.

Channing rolls his eyes, taking another drag from his cigarette. "I've told you, that information is confidential." He softens a bit recognizing my desperation. Letting out a sigh he says, "She never talks about herself or what brought her here. She's just… there. Encouraging, and empowering the other members. She's a pleasure to have in the group."

His words offer a sliver of insight, but not enough. "Can you give me her name?" I ask, knowing the answer but hoping for a miracle.

"No," Channing replies firmly. "Not without a warrant."

I sigh, defeated but grateful for what he's shared. "Thank you anyway, Channing. I appreciate your help." He flicks his cigarette into the grass and heads back inside.

When I arrive at the precinct it isn't long before I receive an email from the lab. I take a deep breath and open it, my eyes scanning the words quickly. Relief floods through me as I read that the hair fibers match a contractor, someone who has a previous felony on his record – a violent attack on a patron in a bar. The contractor has worked on various projects around Booker's house, which explains how his hair could have ended up there. However, to make progress I'll bring him in for an interview anyway.

The subpoena for the Shadow Stalker Updates page is approved and issued shortly after. I immediately forward it to the legal team at Echo, crafting a message that carefully avoids requesting the personal details of the page owner. I don't want to expose the identity or location of the person running the page. What I need is for the page to be removed, and the creator barred from making any more.

In my message, I stress that the page is obstructing justice and that if it isn't removed, legal action will be taken against the Echo platform. My thoughts are interrupted by a knock on the door. It's Captain Walsh. He steps in. "Any updates, Carter?"

"Yes, Captain. The hair fibers found at Booker's scene belong to a contractor who worked on her house. He's got a felony on his record, but it's for a bar fight, nothing that connects him directly to her murder. However, I'm going to bring him in for an interview to determine where he was that night," I explain. "And the subpoena for the Shadow Stalker Updates page has been issued. I've just forwarded it to Echo."

Walsh nods, looking slightly relieved. "Good work. Let's hope Echo responds quickly. The sooner that page is down, the better."

"I agree. It's causing more harm than good. We

need to control the narrative," I reply.

He taps his knuckle against my desk firmly. "Keep me updated. We're counting on you."

"I will, Captain," I assure him, watching as he leaves the room. I turn back to my computer, refreshing my email repeatedly, waiting for a response from Echo. The minutes tick by slowly. I try to focus on other aspects of the case, reviewing notes, but my mind keeps drifting.

Finally, an email notification pops up. It's from Echo's legal team. I open it quickly, scanning the contents. It appears to be an automated email. They've received the subpoena and are reviewing the request. They acknowledge the urgency and assure me they will expedite the process. It's not the immediate response I was hoping for, but it's a start.

I return home earlier than usual, feeling a rare sense of accomplishment for the day. The house is quiet, the late afternoon sun casts faint lighting through the drapes. I drop my keys on the kitchen counter and make my way to the living room, sinking into the couch with a sigh. A few minutes later, I hear the familiar sound of Phoebe's bike tires crunching on the gravel driveway. She must be back from her ride. The front door opens, and she steps inside, her cheeks flushed from the exertion and the cold air.

"Hey, honey," she greets me, setting her helmet on the table and coming over to kiss me on the cheek. "You're home early."

"Yeah, had a productive day," I reply, smiling up at her. "Thought I'd come back and spend some time with you."

She beams with sparkling eyes. "I'm glad. I'll start on dinner." I watch her as she moves around the kitchen, pulling out ingredients and utensils with practiced ease.

The comforting sounds and smells of baked chicken and rice soon fill the house. As I watch in awe, I can't help but think about how lucky I am to have her. Phoebe has always been my rock, my constant in the chaos of this job.

Once dinner is ready, we sit down at the table. The meal is simple but delicious, and we eat in comfortable silence for a while. Eventually, the conversation turns to Booker. "I still can't believe what happened to Booker," Phoebe says softly, her eyes clouding with sadness. "Even though she wasn't always kind to us, it's tragic."

I nod, feigning sorrow. "Yeah, it is. She was a good detective, dedicated to her work."

Phoebe looks at me, "Do you think if they had kept you on the case, this wouldn't have happened to her? Maybe she was in over her head."

"It's possible," I say, choosing my words carefully. "But knowing Booker, she would have pursued her theories no matter what. She was relentless."

Phoebe sighs, her shoulders slumping. "It's just so frightening to think that the Shadow Stalker will kill anyone who gets in their way. I worry about you. What if... you're next?"

I reach across the table and take her hand, squeezing it reassuringly. "I can protect myself, Phoebe. Despite what it looks like, I'm always a step ahead of the Shadow Stalker. As long as I'm on the case, I'm confident I can stop her."

Her eyes search mine, and I can see the fear and concern etched in them. But she nods, seemingly reassured by my words. "Just promise me you'll be careful."

"I promise," I say, giving her hand another squeeze. After dinner, we clean up the kitchen together, providing a welcome distraction from reality. We chat about lighter topics, trying to lift the heavy atmosphere that has settled over us. As the evening wears on, we settle on the couch to watch a movie. Phoebe snuggles against me, her head resting on my shoulder. For a while, I allow myself to forget about the case and the dangers lurking. As the credits roll on the screen, Phoebe turns to me, her eyes heavy. "I think I'm going to head to bed. You coming?"

"In a bit," I say, kissing her forehead. "I'll just finish up here." She heads back to the room, leaving me alone with my thoughts.

CHAPTER 33
AILA

I sit sorting through mail at the kitchen table, sipping on a cup of orange juice. Jaison is lounging on the couch, off for a day. The soft glow of the evening sun casts a warm light over him, highlighting the contours of his face. He's reading something on his tablet, completely absorbed.

"Jaison," I call out, trying to sound casual. He looks up with warm and attentive eyes.

"Yeah?" he replies, setting the tablet aside.

"I was thinking," I say, choosing my words carefully, "how about we go to Foster's Nightclub tonight? It's been a while since we had a night out."

He raises an eyebrow, clearly surprised by my suggestion. "Foster's? What brought this on?"

I shrug, attempting to appear nonchalant. "Just thought it'd be fun. We haven't been out in ages."

He studies me for a moment, clearly searching for a hidden motive. "You sure? I mean, isn't there something else you'd rather do?"

I shake my head, smiling. "Nope. I want to go

dancing. Come on, it'll be fun." I can tell he's hesitant. He knows me too well. He probably suspects I have an ulterior motive, but he doesn't push it.

"You go. Have fun. I'll wait up for you."

"Sure," I say, trying to keep the excitement out of my voice. "I'll go get ready." I head to the bedroom, my heart pounding with anticipation. Tonight, I'm going to reveal myself to Blake Foster as the operator of the Shadow Stalker Updates page. It's a risky move, but I need his help. His resources and connections could be invaluable in taking down the Shadow Stalker.

I decide to wear my new sequin dress. It's form-fitting and elegant, perfect for a night out. I pair it with black leather boots with four-inch heels, hoping I won't regret the height later. I curl my hair into soft pin curls and apply a light layer of makeup: foundation, mascara, and nude butter lip gloss. When I'm finished, I take a final look in the mirror. I feel a mix of nerves and excitement bubbling inside me.

I head down the hall and see Jaison's eyes light up at the sight of me. It's been a while since I've dressed up like this, and I can tell he appreciates it.

"Wow," he says, standing up and walking over to me. "You look amazing."

"Thanks," I reply, feeling a blush creep up my cheeks.

There's a hint of concern in his eyes. "Are you sure you want to go out tonight?"

I smile, trying to reassure him. "Yes, I'm sure. I imagine what a good time could do for my tension lately."

He walks me to my car, opening the door for me. "Be safe," he says, kissing me softly. "I love you."

"I love you too," I reply, feeling a pang of guilt for not being completely honest with him. But I push it aside.

I need to do this. When I arrive, the streets are filled with life. The nightclub is nestled in the heart of downtown Rutledge, surrounded by other tourist attractions and shops. The neon lights of the club are bright, illuminating the night.

Hip-hop music pours out from the club, a heavy bass thumping in the air. There's a long line of people waiting to get in, and I join them, feeling the excitement build. The crowd is a mix of locals and tourists, all eager to experience the renowned nightlife of Rutledge. When I finally make it inside, the dance floor is packed. People are dancing shoulder to shoulder; the energy is intense. The room is dark, with strobe lights flashing and illuminating the dancers in bursts of color. The bar is crowded, bartenders moving frantically to keep up with drink orders.

I make my way through the crowd, feeling slightly out of place in my jacket. Most of the other women are dressed for the warm, packed atmosphere, not the cold weather outside. I head upstairs to the second floor, which is quieter and more relaxed. It's designed for those who prefer a seated setting to enjoy their parties more intimately, though the music is still loud enough to feel.

I find a corner table that overlooks the dance floor and settle in, scanning the crowd below for Blake. Hours pass, the night growing later, and I continue my watch, sipping on a drink to blend in. I take a moment to check my phone for notifications when a man slides into the seat across from me. He has a cocky grin on his face, and I immediately feel nervous.

"Hey there, beautiful," he says, leaning in closer than I'm comfortable with. "What's a sexy woman like you doing all alone?"

I flash my wedding ring at him, hoping it will deter him. "I'm married," I say firmly, hoping he'll take the hint and leave me alone.

He laughs, holding up his own hand to show off a ring. "So am I," he says with a smirk. "Guess we have something in common."

I don't find his comment amusing. "Well, I'm here alone for a reason," I respond, my annoyance growing. "So, if you don't mind, I'd like to be left alone."

He doesn't back off, instead leaning in even closer. I can smell the strong odor of beer on his breath. "Oh, come on, don't be like that. We could have a little fun." I've had enough. Standing up, I reach inside my purse, my fingers brushing against the cold metal of my pocket knife disguised as a pen.

"I said, leave me alone," I repeat, my voice low and dangerous. The guy's eyes widen, and he throws his hands up, backing away quickly. "Whoa, calm down, crazy lady," he mutters before retreating back into the crowd. I watch him go, feeling lingering anger. I sit back down, my heart pounding, and refocus my attention on the dance floor below. It's almost closing time when I finally spot him.

Blake is downstairs at the bar, whispering in the ear of a young woman. She's with a friend, both of them dressed in barely-there outfits. The girl Blake is talking to wears a pink jumpsuit with a plunging neckline that extends down to her belly button. Her friend is in a fishnet jumpsuit.

Blake orders them a few rounds of drinks, and I watch as they giggle uncontrollably, clearly tipsy. They cling to his every word, finding everything he says hilarious. I wonder what could be so funny, but more importantly, I need to talk to him. As the night draws to a close, Blake and the two girls head towards the exit. I realize this is my chance. I dart from my seat, weaving through the crowd and rushing down the stairs. By the time

I make it outside, Blake is already getting into a Rolls Royce with the girls. I watch, feeling a sense of defeat wash over me, as the car drives away.

I stand there for a moment, the cold night air biting at my skin. I've missed my opportunity, and now I'm not sure when I'll get another chance. I head back to my car, flustered. The drive home is quiet, the streets mostly empty at this hour. When I finally pull into the driveway and walk inside, Jaison is waiting for me on the sofa, pretending to be interested in a re-run of the local news. The concern is evident in his look.

"How was it?" he asks.

I shrug, trying to keep my disappointment hidden. "It was okay. Just needed to get out for a bit."

He wraps his arms around me, pulling me close. "I'm glad you're home safe."

I shower and climb in bed, beat. Blake and the young women he left with are on my mind. I wonder if they're safe, if he's someone they can trust. They seemed to enjoy his company. Unveiling the secrets of the victims of this case has me questioning everyone. Though I push the thoughts to the back of my mind and choose peace.

CHAPTER 34
CARTER

I sit across from Jenkins in the small interrogation room, the glowing lights flickering overhead. The contractor, a husky man in his late forties, shifts uncomfortably in his chair. He looks rough around the edges—his hands are calloused, his nails dirty, and his face weathered. He claims his presence here is a mistake, that he had nothing to do with Booker's murder.

"So, Mr. Thompson," I begin, leaning forward, "you said you routinely work on projects around Ms. Booker's house. When was the last time you saw her?"

"A week before she was killed," he replies, a hint of irritation in his voice. "I was fixing some cabinets in the kitchen."

I nod, jotting down notes even though I've heard this part before. It's more about the pressure we apply. "And during this visit, did you spend any time in the bedroom?"

Thompson's eyes narrow. "I go where the work takes me. If there's a project in the bedroom, then yeah, I'd be there."

I exchange a glance with Jenkins before continuing. "You have a bit of an aggressive history, don't you, Mr. Thompson? A previous conviction for assault in a bar fight. Care to explain that?"

Thompson's jaw tightens. "That was years ago. I've kept my nose clean since then. That has nothing to do with Booker."

"Maybe," I say, feigning nonchalance. "Or maybe it does. Booker was a single, vulnerable woman. You saw her regularly. Ever take an interest in her beyond the professional interest?"

Thompson's face flushes red with anger. "I would never hurt her. I respected her."

"Then why was your hair found near her bedroom?" I press, my voice growing harder.

Thompson chuckles bitterly. "Why wouldn't it be? I've worked all over that house. I'm bound to leave something behind."

I lean back, pretending to jot down more notes while I watch him carefully. "This is no laughing matter, Mr. Thompson. You're facing serious allegations here."

He bristles at that, but I can see the flicker of fear in his eyes. "I'm telling you, I had nothing to do with it."

Time for the gambit. "We also found personal items of yours among her belongings," I lie smoothly. "Things that shouldn't be there unless you had a more... intimate relationship." I knew this from my multiple trips to stake out Booker's place.

Thompson freezes, his foot tapping rapidly against the floor. He swallows hard before speaking. "Alright, fine. We were... involved. I loved her, and she loved me. I spent nights there. Maybe I left something behind."

I exchange a shocked glance with Jenkins. "Involved how, exactly?" I ask, keeping my voice steady.

Thompson sighs, his shoulders slumping. "Booker and I were together for years. She was married, yeah, but we found comfort in each other. When her family found out, it got ugly. Her husband filed for divorce, and she lost custody of her kids. But we stayed together."

The pieces start to fall into place. "Her husband and kids didn't know about you initially?"

"No," Thompson says, shaking his head. "She kept it secret. But when they found us together, everything fell apart."

Jenkins speaks up, his voice skeptical. "And you have an alibi for the night of her murder?"

Thompson nods vigorously. "I was working on a project for another client. There's a timestamp on the payment, and the client can verify it. I wasn't anywhere near her house."

I sit back, mulling over his words. His story seems to check out, and if he has an alibi, we're wasting our time. "Alright, Mr. Thompson," I say finally. "We'll verify your alibi. For now, you're free to go." Thompson stands up with lingering anger on his face. As he leaves the room, Jenkins turns to me, "Looks like it's back to the Shadow Stalker," he says.

"Yeah, it does. But we'll get there."

The interrogation room feels colder now. I gather my notes and return to my office. I wake up my computer and see an email from Echo. My pulse quickens. I open and skim through the contents. Echo confirms that the Shadow Stalker Updates page has been removed and cannot be reinstated. That's a win. However, they mention that the page wasn't created with any real information, and the user was using a VPN. They don't have the actual location or IP address of the page owner. They advise us to contact the

VPN provider but note that because the user is utilizing a VPN, they could easily access the platform again using another VPN.

Echo's legal team also explains that there's no way to prevent the user from creating additional pages, but they offer assistance in removing any new pages or content that might pop up in the future. I lean back in my chair, contemplating the implications. On one hand, we've successfully removed the current page, cutting off the Shadow Stalker's primary means of communication. This will disrupt their operations significantly. They'll have to start from scratch to build a new audience and online presence, which is no small feat. On the other hand, there's the possibility that they could bounce back quickly, creating new pages under different aliases.

The department asked me to deliver a speech at Booker's wake after Captain Walsh. I take a deep breath, trying to gather my thoughts and push away the tremor in my hands. Booker deserves a speech that honors her memory and captures the impact she had on our community and the precinct.

I flip through my notes, scribbling a few last-minute changes. I want to make sure I do justice to her legacy.

Arriving at the church, the somber atmosphere hits me. The air is thick with grief. The pews are filled with mourners—friends, family, colleagues. Captain Walsh stands at the front, delivering his speech with a steady voice. As he finishes, he nods to me, signaling that it's my turn. I make my way to the podium, my eyes briefly catching the sight of Booker's lifeless body in the open casket. She looks peaceful, almost as if she's merely sleeping.

Clearing my throat, I begin. "Ladies and gentlemen, thank you for being here today. We gather to remember and honor Detective Cynthia Booker, a woman whose life was cut tragically short. Booker was not just a dedicated member of our precinct; she was a beacon of hope and determination. Her tireless efforts to seek justice have left a permanent mark on all of us."

I pause, scanning the room. Faces are etched with distress while eyes glisten with unshed tears. "Booker was the kind of person who never backed down from a challenge. Her commitment to her work was unparalleled, and she always went above and beyond to protect and serve our community. Her death has shaken us to our core. It has left a void in our precinct and in our hearts that can never be filled. She was not just a colleague; she was a friend, a mentor, and a guiding light for many of us. The impact of her loss is profound, and we are all grappling with the pain and the senselessness of it."

I take a deep breath, feeling the lump in my throat. "We must also acknowledge the dark reality that brought us here today. Booker's life was taken by someone who sought to undermine the very principles she stood for. The person responsible for this heinous act is a coward, hiding in the shadows and preying on the innocent. They have not just taken a life; they have attempted to shatter the spirit of our community. But we will not let them succeed."

The room is silent leaving my words hanging in the air. "Booker's legacy will not be tarnished by this senseless act. We will honor her by continuing the work she was so passionate about. We will seek justice for her and for every victim whose voice she spoke for. We will stand united, stronger than ever, and we will not rest until the person responsible is brought to justice."

I step away from the podium, my eyes meeting

those of Booker's family. They nod, a silent acknowledgement of the pain and the determination to keep fighting. The wake continues with people sharing their memories of Booker, their voices a mix of laughter and tears. I slip out before it ends to avoid staying behind for conversations.

CHAPTER 35
AILA

I find myself in a neighborhood that feels both familiar and alien. The houses are rundown, windows broken, doors hanging off their hinges. The streets are deserted, bathed in the dim light of flickering street lamps. The air is thick with the scent of scattered trash and abandonment. My footsteps echo as I walk, the sound unnaturally loud in the oppressive silence.

Suddenly, I spot a shadowy figure lurking in the periphery of my vision. Panic surges through me, and I start to run. My heart pounds in my chest, each beat a deafening drum. I can hear his footsteps behind me, steady and relentless. The neighborhood around me blurs as I sprint, my only thought is to escape.

I see an abandoned house ahead, its door ajar, inviting me in. Without hesitation, I dart inside, slamming the door shut behind me. The interior is dark and silent, the air stale. I make my way up the creaky stairs. The house feels eerily familiar, like a half-remembered dream from long ago. I reach the third floor, a finished attic with a narrow staircase connecting it to the second floor.

The attic is a snapshot of despair. A worn-out

mattress lies in one corner, in front of a small box TV resting on the floor. Clothes are scattered everywhere, as if the previous occupants had left in a hurry. The sight is unsettling. I crouch behind a pillared wall in the shadows, my body trembling with fear. I cover my mouth to suppress my whines, my breaths coming in shallow, ragged gasps.

I smell a strong, unpleasant odor of gasoline. It seeps into the attic, increasing in intensity with each passing second. My heart races faster, if that's even possible. I peek around the pillar and see the man at the top of the stairs, pouring gasoline with deliberate, measured movements. He flicks a match into the fluid, and flames roar to life, blocking my only exit.

Panic grips me as I watch the fire spread, the heat becoming unbearable. The flames are voracious, consuming everything in their path. I scan the room frantically, my eyes landing on a small window that overlooks the front lawn. It's too small for me to fit through, but it's my only hope. Desperation fuels me as I make my way to the window, but I know it's futile. The fire closes in, the heat scorching my skin as smoke fills my lungs.

I'm shaken from my nightmare by Jaison who's terrified. Tears stream down my face, the horror of the dream lingering in the edges of my consciousness. Jaison pulls me into a tight hug that threatens to crush me. I cling to him, my body shaking with sobs. He doesn't say anything, just holds me, offering comfort.

"Shh, it's okay." he murmurs, his voice soothing. I take deep, shuddering breaths, trying to calm myself. The room around me slowly comes into focus.

"I was trapped," I whisper, my voice hoarse. "There was no way out."

"It's over now," Jaison reassures me, his hand

stroking my hair. "You're safe."

We sit in silence, the only sound being the occasional sniffle from me. The terror of the dream still lingers, but with Jaison here, it feels more manageable. We sit like that for a long time, the quiet of the night enveloping us. Slowly, my heartbeat returns to normal, and the terror of the dream fades into a distant memory.

CHAPTER 36
DIDI

My place is modest but comfortable, decorated with eclectic finds from various thrift stores and yard sales. I like to think it has character; much like me. I sit on my bed, scrolling through my phone out of boredom. The room is dimly lit by the bedside lamp, meant for the book I promised to finish tonight but tossed on the nightstand instead. Hunter's been on my case about reconnecting with Aila. The mere thought makes me roll my eyes. Aila, the goody two-shoes who always had to be the voice of reason, the one who never fit into our wild little trio. I never understood what Hunter saw in her.

My childhood was a mess. Growing up in foster care under my aunt's roof was like living in a perpetual storm. She wasn't exactly the nurturing type—more like the "tough love" kind, minus the love. She was quick to punish and slow to show any affection. Her house was always cold, both literally and figuratively. The only warmth I found was with Hunter after we met in a group home for kids labeled as having "behavioral problems." He had this aura about him, a mix of danger and charisma that drew me in immediately. He was the cool older brother I never had, teaching me how to navigate life's darker corners. We did everything together, from sneaking out at night to causing trouble around town.

As we grew older, we became inseparable, partners in crime and confidantes. Aila came into the picture when we were teens. Hunter saw something in her, some spark that I was blind to. She was the complete opposite of us—straight-laced, cautious, always doing the right thing. Whenever she hung out with us, she complained, clearly uncomfortable with our lifestyle. I couldn't fathom why Hunter wanted to keep her around, why he felt the need to save her. It made me envious, a feeling I hated but couldn't shake.

For Hunter's sake, I pretended to like her, but deep down, I resented her presence. Even now, years later, the thought of Aila makes my blood boil. I see her as a reminder of the life I never had—a stable, predictable one. We've lost touch over the years, and now he's adamant about finding her again. I've tried to discourage him, reminding him of the friction she always brought into our dynamic, but he won't listen. So, when I ran into Aila at the mall a few days ago, I knew it was only a matter of time before they reconnected. And when they do, I'll be left in the shadows again. I'm jealous. Jealous of the attention Hunter always gave her. Jealous that she never had to fight for his approval like I did.

In the mall, she looked different, more confident. She'd grown into her figure, plumping up in all the right places. Her hair was just as gorgeous as before and her flaw free skin irked me with it's perfection. We exchanged pleasantries, but I could tell she saw through my facade. She knew I didn't care for her, but she played along, probably for Hunter's sake. But for now, I have to put on a brave face and pretend I'm okay with it. Because that's what Hunter wants, and I'd do anything for him.

Hunter has been acting strange lately. It's not just his usual level of strange, either. He's fixated on some goal he keeps mentioning in these vague, cryptic ways, like he's on a quest to find the Holy Grail or something. And he wants Aila's help. Not mine. Yeah, that stings. Aila, of all people. I mean, I get it—she's Miss Perfect with her flawless record. But this time, she doesn't even want to help. She's been avoiding Hunter and his grand mysterious mission like it's a group project and she's the only one doing the work. I'd help him in a heartbeat, but I'm left out.

So here I am, lounging on my bed, tossing a rubber ball against the wall, trying not to think about how Hunter used to include me in everything. I remember the days when we were partners in crime. Literally. I close my eyes and a memory floods back.

***

It was a tough winter, and the pantry was emptier than usual. My aunt had been gone for days, on one of her "business trips," which everyone knew was code for "disappearing act." The children and I were trying to stretch the last few cans of soup and boxes of macaroni, but we were down to a packet of saltines and a jar of questionable olives.

Naturally, I called on Hunter. I felt responsible for the children who could not fend for themselves. I was sitting on the floor, back against the wall, when Hunter walked in with that look on his face—the one that meant he had a plan. I should've known then that it was going to be something drastic.

"We're going shopping," he announced, eyes

sparkling with that wild, determined glint.

"Shopping? With what money?"

Hunter smirked. "Who said anything about money?" I felt my heart skip. This wasn't the first time Hunter had suggested something like this, but it was the first time it felt...necessary. Aila was horrified.

"Stealing is wrong," she said, closing her book with a snap. "We can't just—"

"We can and we will," Hunter interrupted. "Unless you have a better idea? Didi hasn't eaten a proper meal in days. Are you going to let that continue?"

Aila's eyes flicked to me, and I saw the conflict there. She hated the idea, but she also hated the thought of me going hungry. Still, she was Aila. Morality and rules were her bread and butter.

"Let's go," I said, standing up. "Before the store closes." Hunter nodded, and we headed out, Aila trailing behind us, still muttering about the immorality of it all. The plan was simple. Hunter would create a distraction, and Aila would grab what we needed. My job was to keep a lookout. Aila ended up being more of a nervous wreck than anything.

Inside the store, my heart pounded like a drum. I kept thinking about how this was our only option, how we had no one to turn to. I watched as Aila moved quickly, grabbing bread, crackers, cereal—anything that would last. Hunter was at the front, causing a scene over some expired coupons. Everything was going smoothly until Aila, bless her rule-following heart, got caught trying to hide some cans of soup under her jacket.

The store owner was this old guy and he had eyes like a hawk. He nabbed Aila, and the next thing I knew, she was ratting us out, tears streaming down her face. "Didi and Hunter made me do it!" she cried. "I didn't want to, but they forced me!" Hunter and I slipped out in the chaos, but the damage was done. Back at home, the argument exploded.

"I can't believe you," I yelled at Aila. "You gave us up just like that!"

She sobbed harder. "Stealing is wrong, Didi! We could have found another way! You should've gone to the food bank, or social services, or—"

"And get separated from my family? End up in different foster homes? No way!" I was shaking with anger. "You don't get it, Aila. You've got your perfect family and your perfect life. We don't have that luxury!" Hunter stood between us, trying to play peacemaker, but I was done. "I'm done with you," I told Aila. "I can't trust you anymore."

***

The sound of the oven timer jolts me back to the present. It's 1 AM, and my frozen pizza is ready. I drag myself to the kitchen, retrieve the pizza, and dig in, eating four slices like it's the last meal I'll ever have. Maybe it's the late hour or the flood of memories, but the pizza tastes like cardboard.

I can't help but wonder what Hunter's up to now, behind closed doors. And why he thinks Aila, of all people, is the one he needs. As I munch on my pizza, I wait to hear back from Hunter.

.

CHAPTER 37
HUNTER

The evening closes in as I fix myself a turkey sandwich with a glass of milk, taking my time as the night drags on. I sit at the table, the sandwich half-eaten, the milk untouched, and stare at the wall. My mind races with thoughts of the night ahead, anticipation curling in my stomach. I finish my sandwich and rinse the plate in the sink. My reflection in the kitchen window catches my eye. My hair is a tangled mess.

I head back to my room to slip into a fresh outfit. Pulling my hair back into a neat ponytail, I tuck it under a black ski mask. The mask is snug against my skin, making me feel like I'm slipping into another identity—one that's colder, more calculated. I put on a black turtleneck and black leggings, both tight-fitting and perfect for moving silently in the dark. My black running sneakers are already by the door, waiting for me. I take a moment to double-check my preparations, making sure everything is in place. I need my gloves, and I'm certain I left them in the top left drawer of the counter near the patio door.

But when I search the drawer, they're not there. I frown, my meticulous mind replaying every moment I had them last. I'm certain I put them there. My attention shifts to the right nightstand in the bedroom, and I find them there, neatly tucked away. It's odd, unsettling even. Did someone move them? Is someone messing with me? But I don't have time to ponder. There's a job to do.

I slip out into the night. My destination isn't far, just a few blocks away. The neighborhood I'm headed to is where the elite live, with sprawling mini-mansions and expensive cars lining the driveways. I walk briskly, my steps silent against the pavement. As I approach my target, a beautifully structured brick home, I take in the details. It sits on a slight incline, the front driveway curving in a U-shape from one end to the other. Neatly trimmed shrubs line the yard, and a Rolls Royce and BMW i8 are parked in the driveway. It's late, and the house is mostly dark, save for one corner light near the left side of the entrance.

I move to the side of the yard, blending into the shadows, and head for a window in the back. I've been here three nights in a row, and I know this window is often left unlocked. Carefully, I avoid the security camera near the entrance, my heart pounding in my chest. When I reach the window, I use a large rock to boost myself up, thrust it open with force, and slip inside.

I find myself in a long corridor with beautifully laminated hardwood floors that shine under the dim light. The air inside is cool and carries a faint scent of teakwood and old books. The walls are adorned with expensive-looking paintings, each one meticulously framed and evenly spaced.

As I creep through the corridor, I hear a voice from a front room, accompanied by the clattering of computer keys. The voice is singing softly along to a song, and I recognize the melody immediately. Keeping my back to the wall, I slide slowly towards the room. My movements are silent, every step measured and deliberate. I've already checked for pets and children in past visits; there are none. The only potential threat between 7 AM and 3 AM is a stocky driver who doubles as security, but he's not here now.

Turning the corner into the study, I see the room lined with floor-to-ceiling bookcases filled with books. The scent of leather and aged paper fills the air. At the center of the room is a large mahogany desk, and behind it, with his back turned, sits the man I've been watching. He has earbuds in and continues to hum along to the song, oblivious to my presence.

I creep up slowly, removing the ski mask as my heart hammers in my chest. Blake, the man at the desk, suddenly stiffens, sensing something. He turns around, eyes wide, and utters, "Phoebe?" Without hesitation, I lift the metal bat I found near the rear of the house and bring it crashing down on his head. The sound is sickening—a dull thud followed by a crash to the floor. Blake crumples and the room falls into an eerie silence.

.

CHAPTER 38
CARTER

The middle of the night finds me sitting in my car outside the apartment, the engine off, and the windows rolled down just enough to hear the sounds of the city. The neighborhood is quiet, the kind of silence that feels oppressive. I've been watching her closely for weeks, learning her patterns, her routines. Tonight, she's dressed in all black, fitted clothing that clings to her form as she leaves her apartment, a ski mask obscuring her features. It's almost laughable how obvious she thinks she's being discreet.

The thing about the Shadow Stalker is that she's incredibly intelligent and thorough, but her actions are steeped in emotion. If I don't bring this to an end soon, so many more people could get hurt. I tried to understand why she was at that support meeting for victims of sexual assault, but when Channing refused to answer all my questions, I hit a dead end. I imagine she's affected by something personal, perhaps avenging a friend or other innocent women who were abused. But right now, her motivations don't matter as much as stopping her does.

I see her start walking towards her destination, and

I know I have to follow her. Quietly, I exit my vehicle, sticking to the shadows as I trail behind her. She's careful, checking her surroundings repeatedly, but I'm quick to take cover each time she glances back. My heart pounds in my chest but determination drives me forward.

She stops at a large single home in Tailor Gardens, a community for the wealthy, the kind of place that should be gated but isn't. The homes are beautiful, each one a testament to success and stability. This house is no exception, its exterior is pristine and impressive. She sneaks around the back of the dwelling, and I follow close behind her, crouching behind a bush to stay out of sight. I watch as she leverages herself onto a large stone and climbs into the home through a window.

What is she doing? This is dangerous. A house this nice is bound to have intense security, an alarm system at the very least. I fear that as soon as she steps foot inside, the alarm will sound, and she'll be arrested and hauled away to the station. But no alarm sounds. The neighborhood remains strangely quiet, the only noise is the occasional rustle of leaves in the breeze.

I wait, nerves on edge, listening for any sign of trouble. Time stretches, each minute feeling like an eternity. When I feel it's been too long, I reluctantly decide to follow her inside. The window is left ajar, and I use it to slip into the house. The interior is dark, shadows pooling in the corners, the air cool and still. I can hear sounds coming from a small room at the end of the hallway— muffled crashes and thuds, followed by a woman wailing.

I move cautiously, my steps amplifying every creak of the floorboards under my feet. I reach the doorway and peek inside. What I see makes my blood run cold. A woman driven by vengeance, is relentlessly beating a man with a metal bat. Blake Foster, a renowned public figure and owner of Foster's Nightclub, lies defenseless on the floor. His body jerks with each impact, and I realize with horror that she's killing him.

My heart skips a beat at the implications of what she's doing. This will make headlines, possibly outside of the city as well. But she's relentless, her face a mask of fury and determination. I have to stop her.

"Phoebe?" I call out, my voice soft but panicky. She doesn't budge, doesn't even acknowledge me. It's as if she's possessed, driven by a force she can't control.

"Didi?" I try again, louder this time. Still no response. Desperation gnaws at me, and I call out, "AILA!" The name echoes in the room, but she remains focused on her brutal task. Finally, I shout, "Hunter?" The name cuts through the fog of her rage, and she stops, turning back to follow the voice she hears.

"Hunter? Is it you? It's me… Jaison." My voice breaks, filled with emotion. I can see the confusion in her eyes, the struggle to place the name.

"Hunter, you must trust me. Ask Aila; you can trust me. We have to get out of here. Now." I inch towards her slowly, my hands outstretched in a gesture of peace.

Her expression softens, tears starting to flow down her cheeks. The bat slips from her fingers, clattering to the floor. "Come… come with me. If you stay here any longer, the police will arrive, and you'll be arrested. We have to go."

She finally gives in, her shoulders slumping in defeat. I retrieve the mask she wore earlier. I take her hand, and we move quickly, slipping back out the window and into the night. We run, our footsteps echoing in the quiet streets, hearts pounding in sync. We don't stop until we're far from the house, hidden in the shadows of an alleyway. I pull her into a tight embrace, feeling the tension drain from her body. "It's going to be okay," I whisper, even though I'm not sure it will be. But for now, we're safe, and that's all that matters.

CHAPTER 39
AILA

The air is stuffy as I approach my apartment, the moon casting a pale light on the empty street. My feet drag a little with exhaustion, each step feeling heavier than the last. I dig into my bag, searching for my keys, the metallic clinks filling the silence around me. Finally, my fingers close around the familiar shape of my apartment key.

As I fumble with the lock, apprehension fills me. I freeze, feeling a looming presence behind me. My breath catches in my throat, and the tiny hairs on the back of my neck stand. Slowly, reluctantly, I turn around. My eyes meet his—the dark, big brown eyes of my relentless pursuer. They are laced with malice, glossy in a way that turns my stomach. He peers down at me, stretching a crooked smirk across his face. His expression screams triumph, as if he's finally achieved his sinister goal.

"Hello," he whispers, his voice low and chilling. I can smell the stale scent of cigarettes and onion on his breath. His eyes are fixed on me, drinking in every detail, savoring the moment. He reaches out and wraps his arms around me, his hands settling on my lower back in a way that makes my skin crawl. He leans in, his lips inching closer to my neck. I feel a wild, frantic need to escape. I remember the sharp tool on my keychain. My fingers close around it, and without thinking, I thrust it into his neck.

The sound he makes is a mix between a screech and a roar, just below deafening. I don't wait to see the damage. I take off towards my car, my hands shaking as I fumble for my phone. I need to call Jaison. He's the only one who can help me now. I slip into my car, my heart pounding so hard I can feel it in my throat. I jam the key into the ignition with trembling fingers. Before I can start the engine, I see him in front of my car, stumbling and weak. His eyes, still filled with that terrifying spite, lock onto mine. Crimson blood oozes between his fingers as he clutches his neck, trying to stem the flow.

The sight of him—those face tattoos, his arms covered in pointless ink, that creepy, large smile lined with rows of perfectly white teeth—fills me with a cold, consuming rage. I glare at him, my foot pressing down on the gas pedal. The engine roars to life, and for a second, he doesn't move. He stands there, defiant, as if daring me to go through with it. But I don't hesitate. I floor the gas pedal, the car screeching forward. The impact is brutal, his body crashes against the bumper, flying into the air before slamming down onto the hood. He rolls off and hits the ground with a sickening thud.

I feel a strange sense of calm wash over me. I exit the vehicle and stand over his limp body, watching as he struggles to breathe. His eyes, once filled with such terrifying life, now glaze over. Blood pools around him, and I can see the life slipping away from him with each shallow breath. His last breath rattles out, and then he's still. Completely and utterly still. The sight should horrify me, but instead, I feel a strange sense of satisfaction. He's gone. Finally gone.

My eyes snap open, and I'm in my bed. The darkness of my bedroom surrounds me. My heart is still racing, and I can feel the sweat cooling on my skin. I turn my head to see Jaison sleeping quietly beside me, his face peaceful, unaware of the terror that had just gripped me.

I take a deep breath, trying to steady myself. It was just a dream. Just another dream. But it felt so real, so vivid; the feel of his breath on my neck, the sound of his voice, the look in his eyes. I sit up slowly, careful not to wake Jaison. My thoughts are jumbled. I slip out of bed and pad quietly to the bathroom, needing to splash some water on my face, to remind myself that I'm safe. I notice then that I'm wearing leggings that are too tight revealing every detail of my figure. Jaison found me in bed in outside clothes and left me. I haven't worn this turtleneck in ages.

I blame my memory loss on my fatigue and exhaustion. My mind is all over the place shoving the prior hours into a blur. The bathroom light is harsh, making me squint as I turn on the faucet. The cold water feels like a shock to my system, grounding me back in reality. I look at my reflection and trace the lines of my own face, trying to shake the image of his twisted grin from my mind.

I remove my black clothing and replace them with a silk gown. Jaison stirs slightly as I slide back under the covers, but he doesn't wake. Lying there in the dark, I can't help but wonder what the dream means. It's not the first time I've had nightmares about him—about the man who's been haunting my thoughts. Each time, the dreams get more vivid, and more terrifying. And each time, I wake up feeling a little more frayed at the edges. Jaison shifts in his sleep, his arm draping over me protectively. Moments like this make me grateful to have a rock through all of this, always there to support me.

CHAPTER 40
JAISON CARTER

I sit in my office, the soft hum of the air conditioning is the only sound breaking the silence. My gaze drifts to the framed photograph of Phoebe and me from happier times, her bright smile and sparkling eyes forever frozen in that moment. I lean back in my chair, letting the memories wash over me.

***

It was years ago, back when I was still early in my career as a detective but already regarded as one of the best in town. Phoebe came into the precinct as an intern, fresh-faced and eager. She had this spark in her eyes, a curiosity and determination that I found both endearing and intriguing.

"Detective Carter, this is Phoebe," Captain Walsh introduced her. "She'll be interning with us for the next few months."

I shook her hand, noting the firmness of her grip. "Welcome aboard, Phoebe. If you need anything, don't hesitate to ask."

Over the next few weeks, Phoebe proved to be diligent and hardworking. She had a knack for details, often pointing out things others missed. One evening, after a particularly grueling day, we found ourselves alone in the break room.

"You've got a real talent for this, Phoebe," I told her, sipping my coffee. "Have you ever considered becoming a detective?"

She smiled, a blush creeping up her cheeks. "Not exactly. Though, I've always been fascinated by solving mysteries." Our conversations grew more frequent, and soon, we were spending more time together outside of work. We started dating but kept it a secret from the precinct. The thrill of secrecy added a certain excitement to our relationship.

However, two years into her time with the precinct, things took a turn. Phoebe was investigated for accessing unauthorized internal cases and files. Cases that were closed, some of them long ago.

"Phoebe, what were you thinking?" I demanded one night after she was questioned.

She looked at me, her eyes wide with fear. "I don't know, Jaison. I just... I needed to know more. Something inside me wouldn't let it go."

I vouched for her, meeting with my superiors to plead her case. I didn't want her reprimanded or, worse, facing criminal charges. In the end, I convinced her to resign to avoid further consequences.

"I think it's for the best, Phoebe," I said gently. "This way, you can avoid any charges and we can move on." Phoebe agreed, but it was around this time that I started noticing changes in her behavior. She'd switch from being sweet and caring to cold and distant without warning. It was then that I learned about her dissociative identity disorder. Her alter, Aila, had a passion for criminology and detective work, while Phoebe held a role as a records clerk.

Hunter, another alter, was a different story altogether. A carefree, risky man who loved living on the edge. Based on my research, mostly involving long talks with her mother, Hunter seemed to surface after Phoebe had an accidental overdose as a teenager, landing her in a psychiatric unit at the hospital for a few weeks. I remember one of our many late-night conversations where she, or rather Hunter, would talk about the thrill of danger and the need to protect those he loved.

One memory stands out clearly. It was a more recent night, not long after Daniel Edwards was murdered in his home. I found Phoebe out of bed in the middle of the night. Something didn't sit right with me. I had assumed she went for a late-night jog, something not unlike Hunter. I even patrolled the neighborhood in my car but found no sign of her. Just as I was about to phone the department, she returned, acting like nothing had happened. On that night, she had a terrible nightmare.

Later, at the home of Hank Easton, I found an earring. It was strikingly similar to the one I had gifted Phoebe for her 29th birthday, yet damaged from the scuffle. My heart sank as realization dawned. I rushed home and searched her jewelry box, finding only one earring. This confirmed my initial suspicions. On the night of Hank Easton's murder, Phoebe suffered from another nightmare. A pattern was emerging.

One evening, while she was in the shower, I took her phone and discovered she was logged into the Shadow Stalker updates page. That's when I knew I had to act swiftly. I rushed to get the page pulled, hoping to throw the department off her tracks. A homeless woman at the building of Liam Harris described a woman who closely resembled Phoebe, just as she had described to Booker. I visited the office of the building's owner and left a check, instructing him to get rid of all the footage.

***

Now I sit frozen in my thoughts with the weight of my actions bearing down on me. I tampered with evidence, covered tracks, and manipulated the investigation—all to protect Phoebe. After discovering that an alter of my wife had been murdering sexual predators in a vengeful reign, I moved swiftly to cover her tracks and throw the department off her scent.

Phoebe had a dream last night where she killed her pursuer, whose description resembled the late Blake Foster. I believe this is the final kill of the Shadow Stalker. I have taken calculated steps to ensure the department never suspects us, and if the Shadow Stalker is out of the way, the case may eventually fall cold.

I feel a strange sense of relief, but a nagging question remains—why did Hunter join the support group? Why Blake, a respected man who is not a listed offender.

I take a deep breath, staring at the photograph on my desk. Protecting Phoebe has consumed my life, but I can't deny my support of her actions. Unfortunately, my partner Cynthia Booker got too close to uncovering the truth. When she threatened to unravel everything, I had no choice but to stop her.

I remember the first time I saw Phoebe, her wide eyes filled with determination and curiosity. I remember the nights we spent together, the secrets we shared, and the love that blossomed between us. But I also remember the darkness that crept in, the alter identities that surfaced, and the crimes that followed.

I step outside, taking a deep breath that fills my lungs with crisp air. I start the car, the engine purring to life. As I drive through rush hour traffic, my thoughts drift back to the beginning, to the first time I realized the extent of Phoebe's dissociative identity disorder. The discovery had been a shock, but it also explained so much—the erratic behavior, the obsession with certain cases, the late-night disappearances.

Hunter, Aila, and Phoebe—they were all part of the same person, yet so different. Each alter had their own personality, their own desires, their own reasons for existing. Understanding them had been a challenge, but it had also brought me closer to Phoebe and made me more determined to protect her.

I pull into our driveway, the house is dark and inside things look still. I sit in the car for a moment, gathering my thoughts. I've done so much to protect Phoebe, but the fear of being discovered never leaves me. My wife, or rather her alter, was the Shadow Stalker. Unknowingly aiding the department in every step to uncover her truth by creating a page for updates. Phoebe doesn't recall the murders. She was not present. Hunter and I have developed our relationship. He refers to me as a friend. I'll take it. As long as I can get all of Phoebe to trust me. Still, every day is a struggle, a fight to keep the truth hidden.

I step out of the car and head inside. Phoebe is asleep in the bedroom. I prepare the living and dining room with balloons and gold confetti for Phoebe to wake up to. Tomorrow is her 30th birthday and lately she's felt more at peace. I want to celebrate her so I purchased a new pair of those white gold earrings with a topaz stone.

I finally climb into bed around 2 AM. As I lie down beside her, I think about the future. The Shadow Stalker's reign might be over, but the scars remain. I hope we can move on, find some semblance of normalcy. But the past is never far.

CHAPTER 41
PHOEBE

I sit by the window on a loveseat in my living room. It's been weeks since Blake Foster's murder made the headlines. The city is still reeling from the shock of losing such a prestigious figure. The police are attributing this to the Shadow Stalker, but they can't figure out the connection. Blake had no criminal history and wasn't a registered offender. They think the Shadow Stalker made a mistake.

The thought makes me shiver. Blake wasn't just anyone; he was familiar, close to home. I stare at his photo plastered across the news on the screen, and a knot forms in my stomach. His wide grin, filled with what seemed like too many teeth, though they were perfectly straight, and those glazed eyes that looked like they harbored darkness and secrets behind them, all make me uneasy.

Memories of Blake flood back, uninvited. My mom forcing a connection between us when we were children. Blake was my half-brother, born from my father's affair. We didn't know each other until grade school, and I never quite took to him. He always struck me as strange, but maybe that was just the distance. He was five years older, and we never ran in the same circles.

I remember seeing him at town events or when he visited my aunt as a friend of my cousin. But beyond these glimpses, there isn't much depth to our relationship. It's all a blur now. I wonder what kind of person he really was. The memories I have of him are fragmented and distant, colored by my own feelings of betrayal and resentment towards my father. But there must have been more to him than the strange, uneasy feeling he gave me.

I recall one summer when I was about ten and Blake was fifteen. We were at a family barbecue, one of those rare occasions when my dad's various families intersected. Blake was standing off to the side, watching the other kids play. I remember feeling a mixture of curiosity and nervousness. He approached me, looking down, his face unreadable. "Hey, Phoebe." There was that smirk.

"Hi," I said, awkwardly shifting from foot to foot. There was a kid who ran by quickly, losing his balance and plowing right into me. The collision sent me tumbling to the ground. Blake snapped angrily, threatening the kid who appeared to be just shy of 12 or 13. I cautioned for Blake to calm down, insisting it was an accident and the kid had not meant to hurt me. It should have been admirable witnessing his willingness to protect his little sister but the mannerisms and threats to a young boy just made him appear as a bully.

We stood there in silence for a moment, the sounds of laughter and chatter filling the air around us. I remember wanting to ask him so many questions, develop a bond. But the words never came. Over time I realized, I had no desire to develop closeness. I hadn't had a brother but I also hadn't needed one.

Still, seeing his face on the news brings a pang of

sadness. Not for Blake, but for my dad, who lost a son. My relationship with my father has been strained ever since I found out about Blake and the other children he fathered with various women. My mom forgave him, but I never could. The thought that I might have more siblings out there, unknown and unknowable, still bothers me.

I push these thoughts aside. Today is my birthday, and Jaison has surprised me with a new pair of earrings. I open the small, velvet-lined box and gasp. The design isn't new to me. Somehow, I misplaced one of these earrings, my favorite pair. Now they're back, and I vow to only wear them on special occasions, not every day like before.

Jaison's voice breaks my reverie. "Happy birthday, Phoebe. I thought you'd like these."

I turn to him, my eyes filling with tears. "Thank you. They're perfect."

He smiles, wrapping his arms around me. "I know how much you loved them. I wanted to make sure you had them back."

I lean into his embrace, feeling a wave of gratitude and love. "I have a surprise for you too," I say, pulling back slightly to look into his eyes.

Jaison raises an eyebrow, intrigued. "Oh? And what might that be?"

I take a deep breath, steadying myself. "You know how I've been feeling tired lately, eating a lot, and putting on weight? Jaison, we're going to be parents."

The look of surprise and joy on his face is priceless. He pulls me into a tight hug, his voice choked with emotion. "This is the best gift ever, Phoebe. I love you so much."

We stay like that for a while, holding each other, sharing the joy of our news. I can feel the weight of the past weeks lifting, replaced by the hope and excitement of what's to come. The room around us feels brighter, more vibrant. The morning light seems to take on a golden hue. I glance around, taking in the familiar sights of our home— the cozy couch where we've spent countless evenings, the bookshelf filled with our favorite books, the photos on the wall capturing moments of our life together. The paintings piling up in a corner.

As I sit back down, my hand instinctively goes to my stomach. The thought of a new life growing inside me electrifies me. The day passes in a blur of celebration and reflection. Friends and family call to wish me a happy birthday, and Jaison and I spend the afternoon planning for the future. We talk about baby names, nursery themes, and the kind of parents we want to be. It feels surreal but in the best possible way. For the first time in a long time, I feel renewed. It's as if an unseen weight has been lifted from my shoulders and replaced by a sense of freedom.

ACKNOWLEDGMENTS

First and foremost, a massive thank you to Doog for those late nights filled with my rambling ideas and your insightful (and sometimes baffling) responses. Your patience was indispensable.

A heartfelt thanks to my beta readers for their sharp eyes and blunt advice. Your honest feedback turned my scribbles into something decent. I promise I took most of your suggestions to heart.

A huge shoutout to the awesome folks in the **Tee Seabrone TeeMates** Facebook group. You guys are the real MVPs for all of your critiques, shares, and for just being awesome cheerleaders.

And to everyone else who supported me along the way—friends, family, and fellow writers—thank you from the bottom of my heart. Your support means everything.

Cheers,

Tee

Newsletter: TeeSeabrone.com
Instagram: Instagram.com/modestee__
Facebook: Facebook.com/officialmodestee
Group: Facebook.com/groups/teeseabroneteemates

REMARKS

Thank you for diving into the chaotic journey of Aila and Carter in *Insomnia*. If their sleepless nights and relentless chase had you staying up way past your bedtime, then my mission is accomplished. I hope you enjoyed the wild ride and that your own insomnia was purely fiction-induced. Here's to more late-night thrills and plot twists that keep us all awake! If the story captivated you, I'd be delighted to hear your thoughts. Feel free to reach out via email at info@teeseabrone.com or leave a review to share your experience.

Stay updated on new releases and behind-the-scenes insights by following me on Instagram and Facebook, and visiting my website at teeseabrone.com. Join the engaging community of readers in my group, **Tee Seabrone Teemates.**

Other titles:

SUFFOCATED (Liv Wright Series)

ABOUT THE AUTHOR

Tee Seabrone is a multi-talented author and fashion designer from Cleveland, Ohio. Her journey into storytelling began in elementary school, where she crafted chapter books that ignited her passion for narrative creation.

In addition to her literary pursuits, Tee is the co-founder of Tian Zevon, a thriving handbag and accessories brand. Through her entrepreneurial endeavors, she found both the time and inspiration to reignite her joy for writing.

When she's not weaving suspenseful tales, Tee can be found cherishing precious moments with her three children and loving husband. With each story she pens, Tee aims to bend minds, evoke deep emotions, and lead readers on exciting adventures.

For updates and to explore more of Tee's work, visit teeseabrone.com.